FORMER CORPORATE
DRONE ADVENTURER
MIZUKI RYOSUKE

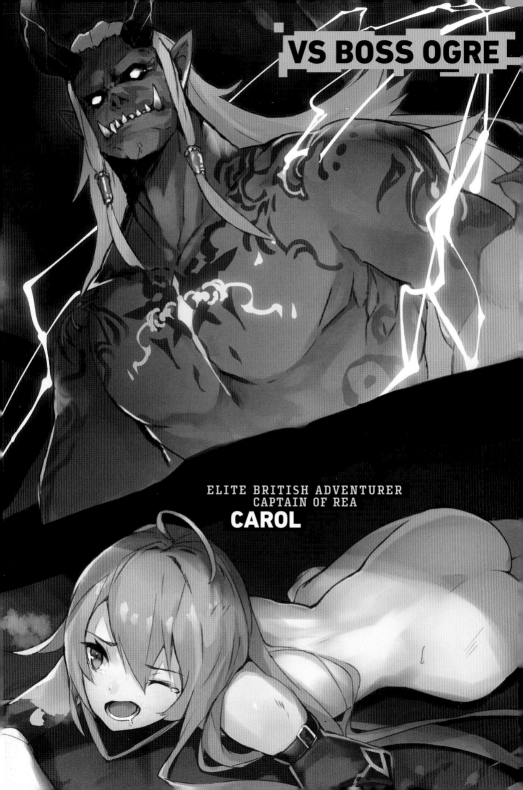

From her neck to her belly button, Shinobu's pale skin was exposed to the Hokkaido air. The hoodie sat over her chest on both sides and none of the important parts came bursting out, but everything in between was fully on display.

CURRENT HIGH SCHOOLER AND YOURTUBER
HIMEKAWA SHINOBU

Modern DUNGEON Capture Starting with BROKEN Skills

NOVEL
01

WRITTEN BY
YUUKI KIMIKAWA

ILLUSTRATED BY
CRUELGZ

Airship

Seven Seas Entertainment

KOWARE SKILL DE HAJIMERU GENDAI DUNGEON KOURYAKU Vol.1
© 2020 Yuuki Kimikawa
Illustrations by cruelGZ
First published in Japan in 2020 by OVERLAP Inc., Ltd., Tokyo.
English translation rights arranged with OVERLAP Inc., Ltd., Tokyo.

Seven Seas press and purchase enquiries can be sent to
Marketing Manager Lianne Sentar at press@gomanga.com.
Information regarding the distribution and purchase of
digital editions is available from Digital Manager CK Russell
at digital@gomanga.com.

Follow Seven Seas Entertainment online at
sevenseasentertainment.com.

TRANSLATION: Ben Trethewey
ADAPTATION: G. Simon
COVER DESIGN: H. Qi
INTERIOR LAYOUT & DESIGN: Clay Gardner
COPY EDITOR: Leighanna DeRouen
PROOFREADER: Catherine Langford
LIGHT NOVEL EDITOR: Cole Moone, Kathleen Townsend
PREPRESS TECHNICIAN: Melanie Ujimori, Jules Valera
MANAGING EDITOR: Alyssa Scavetta
EDITOR-IN-CHIEF: Julie Davis
ASSOCIATE PUBLISHER: Adam Arnold
PUBLISHER: Jason DeAngelis

ISBN: 979-8-88843-195-5
Printed in Canada
First Printing: January 2024
10 9 8 7 6 5 4 3 2 1

Modern DUNGEON Capture Starting With BROKEN Skills

CONTENTS

BEYOND EVERYDAY LIFE

IN EVERY LIFE, THERE ARE SOME WEIRD, BIZARRE, AND eccentric elements—strange, out of this world, abnormal occurrences. But the unexpected oddness that had overtaken the life of one Mizuki Ryosuke—me—and the world at large over the past several years was extraordinary by any measure.

"Mizuki. Goblin, slime. Dead ahead."

So said the blonde-haired girl walking beside me. Carol Middleton, a youth of just sixteen, currently lacked the blue eye color that her Anglo-Saxon genes had granted her. Instead, the whites of her eyes were stained yellow, and her black pupils were split down the middle like a snake's.

Her unusual reptilian eyes detected what lay ahead in the darkness in a way mere human biology never could, and she could extract much more concrete and logical information from the scene before her than simple sight would allow.

She turned to look at me in her red, white, and gold Western-style suit of armor. Her small, soft hand already rested on the sword at her hip. "I can engage them if you like. What do you want to do?"

I continued to walk through the dark cave, lamp in hand. "Nah, I'll do it. Cover me."

"Understood."

We worked together like experienced partners; Carol slowed her walking speed just slightly, allowing me to take the lead by half a pace. Our relative positions took on a new meaning—*forward, rear guard*. I handed my lamp to Carol.

"I'll do it. Cover me."

The line I spoke so casually moments earlier echoed in my mind. It sounded strange.

Cover me. Cover me. Cover me.

Those were words you'd never get the chance to say in everyday life. *I bet someone living a normal existence wouldn't get to say them even once. A normal life doesn't involve engaging enemies, and you hardly need cover from a rear guard to go to work. The only people using words like these on a regular basis are heavily into online games, immersed in their make-believe fantasy worlds, or real soldiers out there living in war zones and fighting every day.*

Such phrases were a part of my life now, living beyond the everyday as I did. This morning, I woke up in my futon in my cheap apartment, ate white rice, natto, and miso soup for breakfast, gazed at the morning fluff on TV with my roommate... And several hours later, I found myself in an unknown cave, *engaged in battle*... And my situation simply required *cover* from a *rear guard*.

Carol gave me additional intel. "Goblin, 10 HP. No physical armor. Slime, 7 HP. 5 points physical armor."

On hearing her words, I made the card binder manifest in my hands with a dull *vwhoosh*.

...My skillbook.

I still don't have a complete understanding of these broken skills of mine. They exist outside of the rules. This book doesn't obey any of the laws that everyone else has to follow. It's a rule breaker I can manifest at will, capable of eliminating anything, and making all kinds of bugged techniques possible.

"'Blaze' should do for both of them. Cast it twice," said Carol.

"All right," I answered, pulling the Blaze skill card from my card binder.

I was completely serious in my actions, but in the end, the intense strangeness of what I was doing began to torment me.

I used to be just your everyday salaryman. *Why am I doing this? A Blaze skill card? HP? Physical armor?! How did I get so comfortable using all this weird and bizarre terminology? How did I stumble out of that safe, comfortable world and stray into this dark and dangerous cave?*

It was to reunite with a certain white dragon.

It was because I encountered a certain fairy.

It was because a certain high school girl pushed herself upon me, and a certain strange neighbor took a liking to me. Because a certain wealthy businessman targeted me, because I fought alongside a certain golden-haired girl, came back from the brink of death with a certain group of elites, and because I came upon these broken skills in the first place.

It's almost impossible to pinpoint the starting point of any life—to untangle the complex twists of fate and fortune in this world and to pick out a single cause. We are all connected, mutually affecting each other, and so everyone and everything shares some responsibility for how things turn out. Nobody alive today is completely divorced from the world at large.

But following those sources back, tracing causes and effects, this was all because *this world went and got connected with that other one.* Going even further back, the responsibility for that incident sat with one crazed man and his own story. But back then, I didn't know any of that. I didn't even know how his story began—I had no way of knowing.

The light from the lamp I handed to Carol made strange shadowy shapes writhe in the gloom. Without even realizing what I was doing, I sped up, taking large bold strides into the cave.

I was about to engage—to make contact with the enemy.

I woke up this morning to my old alarm clock, mixed my natto before I ate it, brushed my teeth, watched TV, got in my car to go to work, and now I'm in the boundary between worlds, facing off against grotesque creatures.

Once this is done, I suppose I'll get back in my car, drive home, eat dinner, watch TV with my dear little roommate, and go to sleep. I might have to deal with that high schooler Shinobu as well... Oh, and do that favor for my new neighbor Heath. From a long-term perspective, there are all kinds of things I need to deal with, all while solving the mysteries of this abnormal fantasy world I've stumbled into, and the broken skills I've happened upon... Nothing to be done about that, I suppose. This is my life now.

I held up the Blaze skill card and took another step forward. I was about to make contact with the enemy that had become a part of my everyday life.

Let's turn back time, shall we?

Where to begin... That day was a fateful one for me, and while it would feel like a safe bet to start with me waking up in bed, that would be a little bit too much of a detour. Everything has a correct starting point all its own. There's no need to start running a marathon the moment you step out of your house into the street—that can wait until you're at the starting line.

My story's starting line was in Hokkaido, Omori City, at the Omori branch of Showa Securities.

CHAPTER 1

IF MY OFFICE GETS SWALLOWED UP BY A DUNGEON, DO I REALLY STILL HAVE TO GO TO WORK?

1

FOUR YEARS HAD PASSED SINCE THE SUDDEN appearance of the dungeons, which were passageways connecting to another world.

Yep, four years ago now... Four years since that first one appeared in New York and swallowed up the Statue of Liberty...

The "NY Dungeon" was still the world's largest on record... And it was as if that dungeon broke the dam. Soon after, mysterious unexplored spaces began naturally popping up all over the world.

They say these dungeons are supposed to be passages to another world, but we've still got no idea what they really are, and how they keep appearing... Not to mention what exactly these places are doing here in the first place. They're practically straight out of some fantasy RPG.

This new frontier for humanity—the dungeons—sparked a flurry of treaties, debates, and agreements between nations over the new resources and rare treasures that lay within, along with many safety regulations concerning their operation. Debates that still raged to this day, as governments struggled to properly manage them... But even so, people were adapting quite quickly to the existence of this new fantasy world.

There's all the world affairs and politics, and then there's me, Mizuki Ryosuke...

"...What the hell happened here?" I blurted out as I stood in front of the countryside branch office I was assigned to.

It had been completely swallowed up by a dungeon.

Love stories tend to come on suddenly, as do transfer notices. They come in the dead of night, like the grim reaper creeping up to steal your life away. In my case, it was an order to leave Tokyo and transfer to a branch in the middle of nowhere, a remote place out in the countryside.

Transfers aren't always unfortunate events, of course. Sometimes, promising employees get sent out to countryside branches specifically to give them higher positions there. Like salmon born in a river who swim out into the open sea, only to return to their homes once they're big and strong—some transfers make it back upstream to elite positions back at headquarters after doing their time elsewhere. In my case, however, it was a clear demotion. Of the many reasons an employee might be transferred, demotion was the one that absolutely had to be avoided.

"Mizuki-kun, transfer. You're off to Hokkaido."

It was the branch manager Uemura, with a grin on his face, who called me in to cheerfully deliver the news. Getting to dispose of an inconvenient subordinate like me for an officially "above-board" reason? He looked overjoyed.

"If you choose to get defiant, and the absences and late notices start piling up over there... You know how that's going to play out, right?"

"I do. Don't worry about me," I replied.

"Do the best you can out there..." he continued. "Don't fight your superiors. Stay quiet, clock in, clock out. Let this be a lesson, eh?"

"I really don't mind this."

I remember saying those words back to him and trying the best I could to put on a brave face as I said my next line.

"You aren't going to use this to try to sweep Nabatame and their 300 million yen under the rug, are you?" I asked.

"...I have no idea what you're talking about."

Once the order came and the whole moving process tore through my life like a hurricane, I arrived in the sticks and discovered that the branch office I was assigned to had been swallowed up by a dungeon.

"*This* is the Omori branch?"

The Omori branch of Showa Securities, to be precise, was a building by the highway about the size of your average fast-food restaurant, though the building itself had at this point, as I said, been swallowed up by the aforementioned dungeon. Its concrete foundation and the ground below the branch had bulged up and eaten the entrance entirely. The automatic doors were crushed open, leading to the dungeon within.

The dungeon must've swept up the building and the ground around it when it appeared.

The rubble sticking out of the ruined building showed tinges of the company's bright purple color scheme. The Showa Securities sign hung on by a thread above the doors, like a pathetic white flag flying over the wreckage.

"What the hell happened here...? I'm not even getting any phone signal," I grumbled at the "out of service area" message on my smartphone.

They did mention there were some carriers that don't get great service up here, come to think of it. Apparently Softbant's a sure thing, so I should switch to them, right? Completely forgot about all that in all the rush of transferring up here...

"They never told me about *this*, though."

Whenever I'm overwhelmed by something unexpected, I can't help but talk to myself. I think I read it's supposed to help reduce stress and anxiety, you know? I also tend to remember meaningless bits of trivia at times like these.

All the achievements of the workers under branch manager Uemura were attributed to *him*, and all *his* failures were the cause of his workers... *But have his bullying tactics really gotten this advanced? When one of your branches gets turned into a dungeon, aren't you supposed to just throw up your hands and call a wrecking company to deal with the mess? Nah, this can't be bullying, it goes way beyond that. I mean, it would be insane for this to happen on purpose... When did this dungeon appear, anyway? Does this branch have dungeon insurance? What happened to all the staff?*

There was no end to my internal flow of questions. I considered calling the relevant authorities, but without my trusty smartphone, the thought just sapped my motivation and made me feel lost.

"So... What do I do now?" I mumbled to myself. "Go inside and clock in, just in case? Heh heh..."

I was half-joking when I said it, but the memories of my transfer came flooding back, and so did the anger, bubbling to the surface.

That asshole, Uemura.

I don't know how much of this is him getting back at me, but does he really think this is going to shake me? He transfers me out to some branch that's just been dungeonized, and thinks that's going to make me panic and run crying back to headquarters? Is this his way of humiliating me one last time? Branch swallowed up by a dungeon or no, I'm getting in to work on time!

With this mysterious mental reflex sprouted within me, and because I wanted to see the inside, I stepped through the bent automatic doors and into the dungeon.

2

COME TO THINK OF IT...ARE ORDINARY CIVILIANS *allowed to walk into dungeons like this without an adventuring license?*

That was what crossed my mind as I crossed the threshold of the Showa Securities Omori City branch.

I don't think there's prison time, but I should at least get fined for this...right? Well, I should be able to explain it to the police, I suppose. I don't think they'd accept clocking in to work as extenuating circumstances for walking into a dungeon, though.

Wait, that's not important right now...

"Heeeey! Is anyone in here?!" I called out once I was a few paces from the entrance. My voice echoed off the walls, ringing hollowly down the seemingly tunneled-out stone of the cave.

'Course there's nobody down here.

A little further in, I came upon a narrow passageway that gently sloped downwards. There was no light, except from the entrance, so I took out my smartphone.

"90 percent charge, huh..."

When I directed my phone's flashlight into the narrow passage, it looked like it went on forever.

So this thing's totally turned into a dungeon already...but when did that happen? A few days ago, maybe? Nah, I mean, even if Branch Manager Uemura was trying to pull one over on me by stopping a report on this from getting through, the Omori branch could've called me directly... Maybe it happened yesterday or something? Were they so busy getting dungeonized they forgot to call?

It doesn't look like we're going to be able to retrieve the company files and client personal information from this place, not in its current state. It might even be that all the files were turned into different matter entirely with this whole dungeon appearing on top of them. There's no way the timecard system's still up and running in here.

All right, I've gone far enough. I had entered the branch half out of curiosity, but now I turned to leave.

I wasn't serious about clocking in to work. I guess the young boy inside of me just wanted to see what these things were like on the inside. I was only after a good story to tell: "Y'know, I once had to walk into a dungeon just to clock in to work..."

I figured I could tell it to clients, I suppose—might get a conversation rolling. *I've taken my look inside now. I should go find a pay phone or something and call the office. I'm an employee, that's all they can expect of me given the situation.*

So then, I turned, and saw that the entrance was gone.

Not just the entrance—that was also my only *exit.*

"Huh?"

The path I walked down just seconds earlier was closed up behind me, a rock wall completely blocking the way back.

"Eh? What the heck?" My confusion had my mind racing.

Hanging around the entrance of a dungeon can't be that dangerous, can it? ...And how did this whole path close up without making any noise?

"Could it be...?" A single thought floated into my mind—a theory that could explain what was happening. "Did this dungeon... literally *just* appear here?"

I had heard these things could be really unstable inside for the first hour after they popped up. As if they don't obey the rules of physics, logic, and causation until they've settled, so the dungeons constantly rebuild, regenerate, and change shape... *There wasn't anyone rubbernecking outside, so I thought everyone knew about this place already. Don't tell me I'm the first one in here...? Did this thing form hours... No, maybe even* minutes *before I arrived?!*

I screamed into the dark cave, despite myself. "You've gotta be kidding me!!!"

The strong glow of my phone flashlight was still my only source of light. My voice echoed pointlessly again off the cramped stone walls of the dungeon. Talking to myself helped me relieve stress. Just hearing my own voice was apparently enough to calm me down.

Now's the time to use that calming power of mine to full effect!

"But, then again, this is *really* bad, right?! How am I supposed to get out?!"

Losing a little composure, I started by kicking the wall beside me. All I succeeded in doing was confirming the walls were basically as solid and thick as the ground beneath my feet.

These cave walls aren't thin in the slightest. Several meters of rock at least...

"I guess I need to find another exit..."

Wiping cold sweat from my forehead, I proceeded down the open path, guided by the light from my phone. After a while, I started to feel terribly out of breath. It came on suddenly, like the oxygen in the air had thinned. Whether it was the air not reaching my lungs, something mental, or an actual change in the air composition, I didn't know...

"Damn it... I'm such an idiot!"

I thought I was safe and could leave any time I wanted! I just came in here for a bit of excitement, and this is where it gets me?! My smartphone... It depends on the model, but I hear they can last seven or eight hours with the flashlight turned on. But then again, it's been about a year since I bought this thing, so how's my little guy going to fare? Six at the most... Five hours maybe? That's my deadline.

I have to get out of this dungeon within the next six hours!

3

"JUST TAKE NOTES."

That's what they told me back when I first joined the company—so many times I got sick of hearing it. I think what they really meant was that I should show I'm ready to pull out my notebook at the drop of a hat—that I'm just that passionate about my work.

In any case, the lesson stuck and was deeply ingrained in me now. There was a softcover notebook tucked into my back pocket, and a several-thousand-yen black pen I bought online that was a bit expensive at my salary. *Two everyday stationery items, and one smartphone... These three things could be my lifelines now.*

"The path's branching again, huh..."

I stuck my phone in my breast pocket and took notes as I walked. The flashlight poked up out of the pocket itself, so I had a steady stream of dazzling light ahead of me, leaving both my hands free. I kept notes of the layout of the cave, drawing a map from the sealed entrance.

Not that I have any frame of reference for this place, though... All I can do is mark which paths I've been down and which ones I haven't.

"There's no point in doing any of this if the dungeon changes shape again, come to think of it..." I mumbled, looking down at my own terrible handwriting and my crude map.

Better than nothing, I suppose. No reason not to. I have to do what I can.

When I came to forks in the road, I chose the paths that sloped upwards—or that seemed to, at least. After some time walking, I heard a cheerful *ding!* sound and stopped.

"Whoa?!"

There were letters burning in the air right in front of me, just floating there.

"Ah... This must be that stat screen thing."

Several things happened to those who came in contact with dungeons, the most noticeable being that an individual's abilities were "statted." Dungeons were believed to have a connection to some other world and worked on slightly different rules. People who spent large amounts of time in dungeons tended to adapt and evolve...

There's a more complicated way of explaining all this, but who cares. I've been statted, plain and simple. I wonder why the stats appear like they would in some fantasy game. I hear it might be some effort on the part of this unknown world to make itself easier for us to understand, like using familiar concepts and stuff. Nothing's known for certain, though, and as of yet, nobody in the world knows the truth about these dungeons. At least I think nobody does, anyway. Give me a call if you do know something. It's an emergency! Oh, right. I'm still in an out-of-service area.

"My stats, eh... Let's see. Kind of exciting to get a look at these."

LEVEL **18**

HP **14**   MP **1**

STRENGTH **27**   STAMINA **13**

WISDOM **15**   INTELLIGENCE **42**

RESILIENCE **22** AGILITY **17**

CHARM **15**

...Hmph.

I couldn't really tell what did what at a glance. I figured I would look it up online once I got out of the dungeon. *My high Intelligence is the only outlier, but I suppose that's just because I've got a reasonable level of education here in Japan... It's probably about the same across most developed countries.*

I walked along as I checked out my stat screen and came to another fork. There didn't look to be much difference between the left and right paths here.

What do I do now...? I pondered, quickly sketching the new details in my notebook.

"I haven't come across any monsters yet, come to think of it..."

Creatures from another world are supposed to live inside these dungeons. I've learned how to deal with the well-known ones like

IF MY OFFICE GETS SWALLOWED UP BY A DUNGEON, DO I REALLY STILL HAVE TO GO TO WORK? 25

goblins and slimes since there was stuff about them on that weird aggregate site I read online once... But I don't think regular people can just solo many of the monsters that live down here.

The clock on my phone told me that almost an hour had passed since I came down here.

Could be I've just had incredible luck not encountering any monsters, but the fact that this dungeon's still generating itself could also have something to do with it. Anyway, I've got five hours or so left before my deadline. And add on the fact that if I find any dangerous monsters down here, it's basically game over for me.

Brutal difficulty. No save points. One life remaining.

Following the left-hand rule, I chose the left path.

Let's see now. When did I first learn about the left-hand rule, anyway? Walking alone in the cramped dark can make such dumb things drift into your head.

Advancing through the suffocating, claustrophobic tunnel, I heard the high-pitched voice of a girl dead ahead.

"Waaaah! I'm sorry! I'm not delicious at all! I know I'm bite-sized, but I really won't taste very nice!!!"

Huh?! Is there someone else down here?! Hearing the scream, I ran.

Could she be someone from the branch office who got dragged under here when the dungeon formed?! All right, I'm not alone after all! Sounds like she's being attacked by something, but if we can group up...!

I put away my notebook and pointed my phone light down the path. Running towards the source of the noise, I burst from a tunnel into a clearer, open area.

"Waaaah! Ah! You there! Hey! You!!! Save me, pleaaaase!!!"

"...Huh?"

There were three goblins in the middle of the room, sitting around a campfire. As for the screaming... It was coming from an individual who was bound to a thin stick, being turned into a chicken skewer before my eyes... A small, fairy girl.

"G... Gob? Gogob?"

"Gob?"

The goblins noticed my intrusion and began speaking (I guess having a conversation?) in a language I couldn't understand. The bound-up, perfectly bite-sized-chicken-skewer fairy cried out again, asking me for help.

"You there! Help me!!! I'm going to be turned into roast fairy at this rate!"

"Huh? *Huh?!*"

As I floundered in confusion, the goblins slowly got to their feet and picked up their long spears from the floor.

Ah, this is trouble. Can't exactly just run either.

It wasn't that I had the urge welling up to heroically stand my ground and save the fairy... It was more that she was the one person I found who could give me some chance, however small, of actually *surviving* this dungeon.

4

THE THREE GOBLINS STOOD BEFORE ME HOLDING primitive spears in their hands—they looked practiced in their use. For me, in terms of weapons, I had a black pen.

Well, that's basically nothing. I mean, this thing did cost me 5,000 yen or so, and its simple and sturdy German craftsmanship is... Oh, damn it. Who cares about that right now?!

The goblins were shorter than me, about the size of your average junior high school student.

But that's just height we're talking about.

Their green-skinned bodies were almost completely nude and covered in a layer of bodybuilder-like muscle. Their ears were also far bigger than a human's, sprouting like wings from the sides of their faces.

Their bodies are actually adapted to living down here in the dark too, unlike me. And I mean, I've heard of people with ears like a buddha's, but those are something else! I think I read about goblin biology online once...

[Sad News] Goblins discovered to be biologically superior to us humans [new goblin research]

1: 20XX/0X/03 (sun) 10:14:56 ID:w78x5fask0

Stamina, strength, sight, smell. I hear they're better than us at everything.

2: 20XX/0X/03 (sun) 10:15:34 ID:IsEkai5HAreM

Age of the goblin, huh

3: 20XX/0X/03 (sun) 10:15:59 ID:Yom4ga35ld

>>2 Underrated post ID

"Whoa!"

As memories of online comments flashed through my head, a goblin's stone spearhead grazed my neck. Whether it was pure luck that I managed to dodge the first attack or thanks to my martial arts experience, I couldn't tell.

I was just in an MMA circle for a little while in college—it wasn't much. I competed in one tournament and got my ass handed to me by a Thai-boxing fighter I met in the first round who used a Muay Thai clinch. My glorious career ended with a lifetime record of zero wins, one defeat.

Uh, that's right! That other website! That's the goblins' weakness...!

178: 20XX/0X/03 (sun) 10:35:44.36 ID:td/35jl54/D.net
>>78 Goblins have low magic resistance, so they're
weak to magic
My friend told me, he's got an adventuring license
186: 20XX/0X/03 (sun) 10:38:12.04 ID:Kl564a84Aq.net
>>178 That isn't a weakness to us lol

Well that was useless! I don't know any freaking magic! No, wait. There's always... That's it!

I turned my smartphone's flashlight on the goblins.

"Gob?!"

"Lin?!"

They shrank back from the intense light.

Goblins live down here in the dark so they're weak to strong lights! I remember seeing that in a YourTube video once!

I barreled through them, knocking them aside, and picked up the stick hanging over the fire, fairy and all.

"Whoa! All right!!! Thank you *so* much! You saved me! I seriously like, owe you my life!"

"Hold on! This is going to be a little shaky!"

I dashed onwards without stopping to look back even once. I heard goblin footsteps behind me echoing through the caves... but I knew that with their small legs, they would never be able to catch me.

"Haaah... Haaah... Th-they won't follow us this far...right?!"

My shoulders heaved as I panted, bent over with both hands on my knees. I ran at full speed through the cave without stopping to think about any of the turns I was making, but I did manage to make it quite far from the goblins' fire. The fairy I saved from becoming their lunch flew in happy circles around me as I stood completely exhausted from the run.

"Oh wow! I'm eternally grateful! Seriously, like, you saved my life back there! They were just awful! If you were one minute later, they would've turned me into a salted fairy skewer!"

"Ahem... So you're a fairy?" I asked.

The palm-sized fairy stopped in the air in front of my nose. "Yep, that's right! I'm a fairy!"

"Uh... Do you have a name or something...?"

"Hmm, hmm... Humans want names right off the bat, I see... Well, call me whatever you like! Or Kessie if you aren't sure."

"All right, so Kessie then. I'm Mizuki."

"Itsuki-san, I see! So nice to meet you!" she said.

"No, Mizuki."

"Nizuki?"

"Mi–zu–ki!"

"I–zu–ki?"

"*Mi!*"

"That sure sounds like a boring name," she replied. "And it's so difficult to say too! How about Zukky?"

"Yeah, fine," I answered, giving in.

The fairy seemed to like the way "Zukky" sounded; she hummed the name to herself musically, then cackled with laughter.

"So, like, er... You can talk, then?" I asked.

"Of *course* I can talk," Kessie said. "What a silly question. Silly as silly can be! *'Does it get wet when it rains?'* is coming next, is it? What a pathetically stupid thing to ask, really!"

"Well, I mean..."

I don't think any creatures have been discovered in the dungeons yet that are intelligent enough to speak to. If this fluttering little palm-sized fairy isn't some figment of my imagination brought on by extreme stress...then this is the discovery of the century, right?

"Huh, wait a minute..."

"What's the matter, Zukky-san?"

"How, er... How can you understand Japanese?"

"Oh, so you noticed! You're a low, nasty, pathetic human, born bound to the material world, but you've done so *terribly* well to realize it, Zukky-san!"

"Do you really have to talk so much? Like, *so* much?"

Kessie flew about with her semi-transparent butterfly-like wings, laughing in amusement. "Hmm, hmm. We fairies are terrifically tumultuous and absolutely astonishing creatures, and there's so much about us I'd like to explain to you! But before all that, Zukky-san, don't you have anything more pressing on your mind? Don'tcha, don'tcha?"

"Ah, you're right. Well spotted."

"We fairies have no difficulty understanding the thoughts of inferior material beings! It's all crystal clear to me!"

"Do you have to badmouth me every time just to get the words out?"

At that, Kessie flipped herself away from me, and darted off down the path. "Come now! You saved my life, so I'll give you a little guidance in return! This way, human. Catch me if you can!"

"R-right. This way? This is the way out?!"

5

"**O**H MY, I'VE BEEN WANDERING THIS PLACE FOR AN absolute *age*, you know! I'm so glad I'm finally going to be getting out!" said the fairy, turning to face me as she led me through the cave.

"So are we close to the exit?" I asked.

"Not only close, but barely a hop away! It's only a little further, a teensy, tiny li'l bit! The exit should be forming just up ahead!" Kessie said, then laughed again happily. She really did look like a little girl—just a palm-sized one with wings growing out of her back.

Her body's got this faint glow to it... And, er... She also isn't even wearing a single scrap of clothing, huh? She's buck naked—there, I said it. Makes me think of a certain kind of collectable figures, given her size... When she's flying right in front of me with her back facing me, I can totally see her perky little butt. If she turned and faced me, I bet I could totally see all kinds of other stuff. I mean, I feel bad for staring and all...but hey, I can't help being interested in what I'm interested in.

"Ohh... It's been so long! Feels like it's been four long years since I got trapped down here in this dark, cramped, sprawling dungeon! Just a feeling though, *obviously*!"

"Four years?"

Wasn't it four years ago that the first dungeon appeared in our world? What could that mean... I feel like I could puzzle something out, but my brain isn't working right at the moment. All this walking around and sprinting away from goblins is making my legs hurt, and I'm aching in all kinds of other places too.

"Oh?!" Kessie twitched, noticing something up ahead. She flew off down a passageway.

"Wh-what is it?! Hey, don't fly so far ahead!"

"There it is, it's here, it's here—! I just got a *feeling*! I'm a sensitive fairy, see? My fairy sense is tingling like *crazy*!"

"Is it the exit?!" I called to her up the winding path.

"Yep! One dungeon exit coming riiiiiight uh..."

A moment later, Kessie floated back around the corner towards me.

"What'd you see?! Is there an exit there?!"

"Uhm... Well, about that..." She scratched her cheek, looking a little embarrassed. "We... We should go search for a different exit!"

"Huh? How come?"

"W-well uhm. I'm just not in the *mood* to take this exit, you know?"

"...What the heck?"

"I-it's okay! I know it took me four years to find *this* exit, but four more short years of wandering and I'm *sure* we'll find another one!"

"Hey look, I can't wander that long. Think about the situation that puts me in, won't you?"

I tried to walk past to look around the corner, but Kessie grabbed me by the shirt.

"Whoa! I really don't think you should look! Nope! I sure think *not looking* would be for the best!"

"Huh?! Why?!"

"It's better for your mental health to leave hope intact! It's *definitely* better this way!"

"Come on, I can't kid myself like that," I countered. "I'm at 40 percent battery here."

"Ahh! Don't look! You really shouldn't!!! You're an inferior human. Your mind is feeble, Zukky-san! I only just found you, so I can't let my only conversation partner have a mental breakdown so soon!!!"

The naked little fairy screamed, but she was so weak I barely felt any resistance when I shook her off. Poking my head around the corner...I saw a huge cave formed of softly glowing crystals. The temperature there was cold, so ice covered the ground and the walls. It even looked like it had snowed in there. The cave slanted upward to the left and right, and there were holes at the peaks of those slopes through which the sun seemed to be shining in.

"All right! So this *is* an exit after all! ...Huh?"

However, my joy lasted only a brief moment. In the center of the cave, backed up against the wall, was a huge creature, coiled up in sleep... Something powerful that I saw countless times before in RPGs.

It was a dragon, enshrined in the heart of the cave.

That's, like, obviously one that uses ice attacks too. This is one of those bosses that's meant to punish players that didn't grind enough levels before reaching this point, and it'll smack them down into the depths of despair. This is the kind of guy who teaches young men to level, to prepare for combat well, and to save before they start a fight, huh...

I looked up towards the light, and my body froze. Silently yet quickly, I walked back the way I came, crouched to the floor, and held my head in my hands.

"...I shouldn't have looked...!" I mumbled.

"That's why I *told* you not to! You dummy!!!"

CHAPTER 2

THE JAPANESE SALESMAN WHO ALWAYS GETS HIS CONTRACT VS THE DRAGON WHO BASICALLY STRAIGHT-UP KILLS HUMANS ON SIGHT

1

I SAT ON A ROCK SOME DISTANCE AROUND THE CORNER from the cave where the dragon was sleeping and consulted Kessie.

"Do you think we'll be able to do something about that dragon?"

"Of course not!" she said. "What are you even saying?!"

"I mean, that thing's asleep right? Can't we just creep in, then creep out of this place?" I asked.

"It *looks* like it's asleep, but the moment it detects us, it'll wake up and kill us in an instant. One puff of that icy breath and we'll be frozen solid, cracked up into ice cubes, left as frozen chunks of meat buried inside those piles of snow for the rest of eternity!"

"Thanks for all the grisly details..."

She doesn't try and soften the blow, huh—she even came at me with a knuckleduster to tell me that up front... But it does help me get an accurate understanding of the situation at times like these.

I propped up my head with one hand on my cheek. "How far away's the other exit?"

"So far away I can't even detect it! I wandered four whole years just to finally find *this* one... And then I got so excited those goblins managed to capture me."

"Then we *are* going to have to get out this way after all..."

"Don't you have any skills or magic, Zukky-san?"

"Of course I don't. I work for an investment bank."

"An investment bank? What kind of combat job is that?"

"It's a *sales* job," I explained.

Kessie pressed me further. "Well what kind of *skills* do you need for that?"

I feel like we're kinda talking past each other here, but I don't even have the strength left to correct her.

"Sales and finance skills, I guess?"

"Ah... So you only have Interpersonal and Merchant-Type Skills, I take it. Wow, you're completely useless, aren't you?" she said.

"Don't forget where you'd be *without* this useless human, fairy skewer."

"This *fairy skewer* is the one who led you to this exit, you know?"

"Ugh..."

We sighed in unison.

"Can that dragon talk?" I asked.

"I think so, yes."

"Seriously?!"

Kessie shrugged at my surprised reaction. She looked exasperated. "Well of course it can. That being is on a different level than us, and great beings can do all that lesser ones can. How would an inferior human ever be able to do something their superior, a dragon, could not?"

Even so, I felt like I had found a single stream of light in the darkness. "So I could get through to that thing...? There are a bunch of ways I could make this work!"

The scariest people in the world are ones you can't even talk to! Like those roamers of the forest, the absolute worst things to come across in the woods... Bears!

Imagine, if you will...

"Hey, wait a minute. I have a wife and children. Do you mind not killing me please?"

"All right, fine. I'll let you go. Have a nice life, buddy."

"You sure?"

"Yeah. I'll just go get some salmon down by the river."

I could never be scared of a talking bear, I reasoned. *There are all kinds of ways to deal with someone if you can get a dialogue going!*

"Why would a dragon ever speak with a lowly human like you, Zukky-san?"

"But fairies are superior to humans and *you're* still talking to me, right?"

"Not even I could speak to that thing. It's a *dragon*! You did see it, didn't you? In terms of mana, and basically everything else, it's on a whole different level. I'm just like a sparkling little jewel. A small, fragile fairy, that's all I am...!"

Kessie stopped, suddenly seeming to realize something. "Wait... What's that dragon doing here anyway? They're supposed to live way, *waaay* down deep in the very bottom of the dungeon."

"Really?"

I figured that made sense. *It's been a long time since the government, the army, and then citizen adventurers started exploring these dungeons...but I've never seen reports about dragons. Yeesh, how many more world firsts am I going to stumble into today? Or maybe there are people who encountered dragons before, and it's just that nobody's lived to tell the tale?*

"In any case," she said, "dragons aren't supposed to sleep next to dungeon entrances."

"It does seem a bit harsh to put the boss fight two seconds from the door... You think there's a reason that thing's waiting there?"

"Hmm... Well, maybe..." Kessie put a hand to her chin in thought. "...It might have been running away from something bigger and ended up here...?"

I decided to bring us back to the topic at hand. "Anyway, so... I *can* talk to that dragon then?"

"I'm sure you *could*, but I wouldn't recommend it. You wouldn't be interested in talking with a *fly*, would you, Zukky-san?"

"Yeah, I think I would. It'd be such a surprise that I'd want to know all about the little guy."

"That's not what I'm getting at. You do get what I mean, don't you?" she asked.

"What do dragons do for fun, anyway? What do they like?"

"You're being *incredibly rude* to dragons right now."

"C'mon, I'm being serious here!" I said. "What do you think they'd be interested in?"

"Hmm... Well I suppose... Huh?" Kessie thought about it for a while then caught herself and stared up at me intently. "You aren't *really* thinking about negotiating with that dragon, are you...?"

"Of course I am. I'm a salesman."

After my strategy meeting with Kessie—and fixing my tie, checking over my general appearance—I walked into the cave where the ice dragon was sleeping. The cold air gave me goosebumps all over. Kessie explained that it was because the dragon was creating a barrier around itself that covered the whole cave with its element.

So this is how it marks its territory.

The moment I stepped into the cave, one of the sleeping dragon's eyes snapped open. The creature's reptilian legs were buried deep in the snow. There was a rumbling sound, as if some great stone statue was just coming to life and starting to move of its own accord. Along with the intense pressure of the thing's presence came a raging, chilly wind. I even felt the moisture in my nostrils freeze.

"..."

I stepped back in fear, and the dragon glared at me in my blue business shirt and tie, sizing me up. Without a word, it opened its mouth wide and began forming condensed ice in the back of its throat, preparing to fire.

"W-wait a minute, please!" I called out.

The dragon showed no hint it noticed I was speaking—as if I was such an inferior being that my voice didn't even reach its ears.

Oh crap, oh crap, oh crap! Can it really hear me?! Does it actually understand?! But I don't have any other choice now I'm here!

As the dragon lazily gathered the necessary ice to blow me and everything around me away, I screamed the words I'd come there to say.

"You... I'd like to consult with you about the management of your important assets!!!"

The dragon suddenly froze up, sucked in the mysterious energy it had been building, and gulped it down. It completely swallowed the icy breath that had been about to freeze me solid and smash me into ice crystals.

<Asset management...?>

The dragon's voice was intimidating, transmitting itself directly into my brain. Never in my life did I expect to hear those words from a white-scaled dragon.

All right! It took the bait! Kessie was right!

I straightened my back to get ready for the real deal. I was going to try to win this dragon over.

"Nice to meet you! My name is Mizuki of Showa Securities!"

<I have no interest in your name...>

"My apologies!" I stuck my head down and prepared to move right on to my next line.

The basic, cornerstone, fundamental heart of any sale was communication—having an actual conversation! *It doesn't matter if you give a bad first impression, or they reject you right off the bat. Just so long as the conversation's still going, the sale's in progress! Right up until the last moment!*

"But, if I may!" I continued. "I have served a great many customers, caring for their precious finances and managing their investments. I am an experienced professional in the field of asset formation and management! This may be presumptuous of me to say, but with regard to your many assets—the many treasures you must guard as a great dragon—I believe I can offer some advice as to how you might put them to good use!"

This was the greatest gamble of my life, using the securities sale skills I had been polishing since my days as a rookie. *Let's see if this dragon's going to bite at a good old-fashioned Japanese sales pitch!*

2

A S I FACED OFF AGAINST THE DRAGON, I REMEMBERED my conversation with Kessie.

"Are you listening? Do you know why dragons live in caves like that one?"

"Nope, no idea."

"Nuh-uh! Sorry!"

"I just *told* you I don't know."

"I meant you're a *sorry* excuse for a human, Zukky-san."

"Haven't heard that one before," I said.

"If you don't know, allow me to inform you!" Kessie said smugly. "They're protecting their treasures!"

"Treasures?"

"Yes! Glittering gemstones! Rare and valuable items aplenty! Dragons have a habit of bringing those items into the dungeon and hiding them right in the middle to protect them from others!"

"They're starting to sound kind of cute," I mused. "But hey, you're right. That's how it works in games too, I guess."

"What's a game?"

"Ah, never mind. Sorry, didn't mean to throw you off." *There's a big gap in knowledge between me and Kessie, huh.* "Anyway, go on," I urged her.

"In other words! What are dragons interested in, you ask...? One thing, and one thing only—their own treasures! I mean they're the strongest, most perfect beings ever, and they're immortal to boot, so they don't have other interests, or really *anything* else to worry about!"

"Treasure... I see! Assets, then! They've got assets!"

"Indeed!"

"And those are my specialty!" I said.

Kessie regarded my expression of confidence with a skeptical glare. "Specialty or not... This is *clearly* still a suicide mission in my eyes, you know?"

"No... There's a way to break through this situation! It's all to do with psychology!"

"*Psy-calla-what...?*"

Back to the present. The scaled dragon, who could easily kill me with one whiff of its icy breath, narrowed its eyes at me.

<Asset management...?>

"That's correct! My job is to provide proper management of the assets which my customers possess!"

<You... You are no thief here to rob me of my wealth...?>

"Not at all!" I said confidently, despite the cold sweat on my forehead.

I can feel it... This dragon is interested...! It's just like Kessie said, this really is all it's interested in!

In general, a person's worries could be roughly divided into four main categories, making up the acronym "HARM"—health, ambition, relationships, and money. The poor creatures of society worry about those four things for our whole lives, of course...but my job as a salesman was to get in there and sell, of course.

My specialties might've been securities and financial assets, but that didn't mean the "money" part of the equation was all I dealt in. Whenever someone planned their financial future, it so often involves old age care, worries about their health, marriage, and so on. My job was to encourage clients to build assets that take all of that into account, and to support them on their way!

This dragon's main worry and chief interest just happens to be... money! Which also happens to be my greatest strength! I never expected I'd have to use these techniques on a dragon, but... Well, what does it matter?!

<Hmph. Such impudence.> The dragon looked down on me from above. <Why should I seek the advice of one so small? My fortunes are safe and secure as long as I remain in this place.>

Hmm... Sure seems like he's shutting me down without a shot in hell at getting through to him...but this works just fine for me! I mean, according to Kessie, it's a miracle this dragon is even talking to a pathetic little thing like me in the first place. He's definitely interested in the topic and just pretending not to be. Also, the smarter someone thinks they are, and the more intelligent they actually happen to be... the more room there is to change their mind!

"But, well... I see there have been quite a few changes around here of late." *You know, the laws of physics shifting as this place continues to generate around us...all kinds of things, really.*

<So what?> the dragon replied.

"Have you not faced any dangers in recent days, perhaps? Though I'm sure a dragon of your stature would have no issue handling such matters..."

The dragon's scales twitched, and the atmosphere tensed around me. It was a subtle shift in the mood, a slight change that I would no doubt have completely overlooked when dealing with a human. *But the imposing aura around him, his presence! He's such a powerful creature it's as if the air bends around him at the smallest change in his emotions! This huge guy's got some idea of what I'm getting at!*

<Do you mean to taunt me, cretin?> The dragon was angry. *<Implying that I fled the center of this labyrinth to pitifully take up residence here at the surface of this place?>*

Bingo...!

I clenched my fists, feeling the pressure of the dragon's presence towering over me. *It's just like Kessie thought! He used to live deep in this dungeon... But some threat chased him out, and he moved up here! He knows what it's like to have your life and the treasures you care about put in danger!*

"Not at all! I meant nothing of the sort!"

<Enough. Now I will freeze you and break you to pieces while you still live! You may remain there in the snow and regret for eternity the way you sneered at me...!>

"I'm an asset management professional, you see! I'm sure I can be of use to you!" I screamed back as loud as I could. "If you kill me, right here, right now, you'll lose me forever! And with me, you'll lose the techniques I have for ensuring the safety of your fortune!"

How about it...? I stood in silence after that and swallowed. My throat was dry.

Behavioral economics, prospect theory... When seeking benefits, people tend to prioritize seeking gains that are most assuredly obtainable. Instead of pitching *"this product is great in all these ways,"* and selling its advantages, buyers are more likely to bite when you mention the *dis*advantages—*"here's what will happen if you don't buy now!"*

But this dragon was clearly no human. *As a salesman, it's more effective to push dangers that advanced age might pose without proper asset management than promise future gains...especially since he's experienced it before as well! The real fear of losing his precious treasures is his greatest concern. I'm presenting a situation where I can protect all of them—and all he has to do is not kill me! I'm not actually sure if I can give him any advice, but that's a problem for future me and my improv skills. For now, if I can just turn this dragon into a client and get over this first hurdle...!*

The white dragon made to open its huge mouth once more, but then paused for a second, glaring down at me. <*...I care not, child...*>

Ah.

Ah...

I stood rooted to the spot, my mind going blank. *It didn't work then, huh... I risked my life on this deal, but it didn't go through.*

Faced with death, I felt strangely ready to give in. *Damn it. They could shuttle me off to the countryside, do whatever they wanted to me, and I swore I would claw my way back, but now...*

Then, it happened. There was a whoosh of fluttering wings from behind me, and something tiny darted up towards the dragon.

"W-w-w-w-wait, please! Oh, noble dragon!!!"

It was my naked, palm-sized fairy friend, who had been hiding by the entrance to the cave peeking in on the proceedings.

"K-Kessie?!"

"Wait!" she cried. "T-t-t-two seconds, if you would! Noble dragon! If you could please allow this inferior, vulgar, *pathetic* moron just a moment of your time—!!"

<*...Hm?*>

Her small frame floated in midair, wings flapping furiously, as she did a dexterous little full body bow with her head to the ground absent below her feet.

"Oh boy! I did stop him, I really did!!! I tried super hard to hold him back! Please, forgive him for being so rude! Oh, *please* forgive him!!!" She brought her hands together, as if in prayer, and rapidly bowed down over and over in time to the beating of her wings.

"Ahem! This idiot saved my life a short while ago! I was about to be turned into a salted fairy skewer, but he *rescued* me! That's right! The other races are base and low, but he's probably one of the good ones at heart! Or I think so, anyway! Please, if even for a moment, if you could just listen to what he has to say! I beg of you, please! I'll do anything you ask!!! And if you're going to kill him, will you at least spare *me*?!"

Hey, what was that last thing?

In any case, the dragon saw Kessie floating in the air before him, bobbing up and down in motions so fierce and fast that it was half prostration and half punk rock headbanging...

He closed his mouth. *<...Hmph. If you so fervently insist. I suppose I have no choice.>*

"Huh?"

"You mean it?"

My jaw, and Kessie's for that matter, dropped.

The dragon cleared his throat with a cough, and his breath froze the moment it left his mouth, falling as snow around us. *<Well... Perhaps I was being overly stubborn about this... Hmm.>*

"Huh?"

"Seriously?"

<I have no interest in it, of course, but go ahead and inform me of this method you have for ensuring the security of my treasure. Just in case. But I am not at all intrigued by the prospect, you understand? Regardless, be detailed if you will. Allow me to show you my pride and joy...a few of my precious treasures, as a special treat.>

Kessie turned to look over at me, grinning. "Hey, hey! Is this that psychology thing you were talking about?"

"Yeah! Let's call it the *high-speed desperate prostration effect*!"

3

"**F**IRST...MIGHT I INSPECT THE TREASURES YOU currently have in your possession, sir?"

<Hmph. Very well. I suppose I will allow it...> There were hints of pride in the white dragon's tone as he moved his huge body aside to reveal the riches stacked up behind him.

"Whoa! Amazing!!! Noble dragons really are on another level!" Kessie was out of her mind with excitement, floating about in front of the glimmering mountain of gold and silver.

Seeing her reaction, the dragon's mood seemed to improve as well. *<Why yes, of course.>*

As for me...I spotted a conspicuous-looking white box in among the mountain of treasure and grimaced. "Oh. That's..."

<What is the matter, human?> the dragon asked, noticing the look on my face.

"A-ah, it's nothing! Well, ahem... What is that? The white box... It interests me... Or, uh... I mean that it looks so stunning!"

<Oh, the white box has caught your fancy?>

"Yes, well... That particular one..."

<You have good eyes for treasure—for a human.> The dragon picked the box up and rubbed it lovingly against the scales of his cheek. *<I found this one quite recently. It's my new favorite, in fact.>*

The commanding voice echoing in my head was long gone, replaced with a cutesy tone reminiscent of someone stroking a cat.

<The durable yet smooth craftsmanship... The glowing, shifting geometric patterns on its surface, and the intricate spell cards slotted inside... Everything about it is exquisite! Oh yes, what a fine discovery...>

He deftly took one of the thin cards in his claws and showed us how it could move in and out of the machine. There was a clicking sound as the card entered, and then it emerged with a symbol printed on the front.

<Behold this intriguing mechanism,> the dragon started. *<I believe it is some kind of magical device for impressing marks upon these pieces of paper. What do these symbols mean, I wonder...? How very interesting... The mystery of it all.>*

I somehow managed to keep myself from crying out in frustration as I watched the white dragon blissfully push cards in and out of the white box in his claws.

That's just a timecard machine! For clocking into work! Everything must've been scattered down here when this dungeon swallowed the branch... Ugh, that's not "durable yet smooth craftsmanship," it's just white plastic! Those so-called shifting geometric patterns are a digital clock! The spell cards? Those are time *cards! And that's Kakuta Eiichiro's card, whoever the heck that is!*

"What's wrong, Zukky? Do you know what that is?" asked Kessie.

"Y-yes! I do indeed!" I said, trying to put my confused brain back in order. "H-how fortunate! You're incredibly lucky that you became my client when you did!"

<What is it?> the dragon asked.

"I know all about this particular device, you see!" I said confidently.

<Oh ho, is that so? I should have expected nothing less from a self-proclaimed asset management professional.>

"In fact, unless something is done soon... This device will cease to function!" *Yeah, it'll run out of batteries!*

For the first time since I laid eyes on him, the dragon looked a little flustered. *<What?!>*

Hey, this guy's kind of cute.

<Wh-what can be done?> he asked. *<Does it require mana of some kind?>*

"No... The device requires *batteries*, which are a special source of energy," I explained.

<I see, I see... And without these 'batteries' you speak of, how long will it continue to function?>

I thought for a moment. "One month, if that...I believe..."

<Just one month?! Truly?!> the dragon cried out. His reptilian eyes narrowed in evident sorrow. *<Such a fragile, fleeting piece of treasure... It saddens me deeply. What a cruel trick of fate it was that it should come to me...!>*

"B-but wait! Don't worry!" I interjected. "I can provide you with batteries from the outside world!"

<You can?! Do so, human! Bring me batteries, and I will reward you with just compensation!>

"L-leave it to me! Looking after the assets of my clients is what this job is all about!"

"Whoa! Awesome stuff, Zukky-san!" From Kessie's high-spirited comment, it sounded like her opinion of me had improved.

<Oh, that is such a relief. I am glad to hear it. What a dangerous thing indeed. Humankind may sometimes be worth listening to after all.> The dragon looked much more at ease. He turned around with a colossal rumbling sound and began searching through his pile of treasure. *<Hmm, hmm... Now where did I put that? When I escaped the black-clothed...I mean, when I decided to move up here, it must've gotten buried... Oh, here it is.>*

The dragon pulled out what appeared to be a small treasure chest from his mountain and set it in front of me. *<Human, promise to take this with you.>*

"I-I will!" I stammered. "I promise!"

<That chest is a small favor of my thanks. You may have it.>

"Huh... Are you sure?!"

"What?! Really really?!" cried Kessie.

The long-necked dragon nodded at us both. *<Yes, yes. This appears to contain spell cards with skills sealed inside, but I have no use for it. I kept it in my collection because I am fond of the box, but nothing more.>*

"Th-thank you so much!" I picked it up and then eyed one of the slopes of the cave that led up and out of here and into the sunlight. "Then...might we be excused to return to the outside world and procure those batteries for you?"

<Aha, my apologies for the trouble. Go. Bring back as many as you can carry.>

I began to walk up and out of the dungeon—hearing the dragon's voice from behind me just once more before I left.

<Come to think of it... What purpose does this white box serve? What is its nature?>

I turned around to answer him. "That device controls time."

<Controls time, you say?! Hmph. An exceedingly lofty purpose— befitting of a treasure indeed!> the dragon snorted, satisfied by my explanation.

At my company, that device controls the precise time at which employees arrive at and leave work. See? Not a lie at all.

When I left the dungeon, everything outside looked just the same as the way I'd left it. I tucked the treasure chest under my arm and checked my phone.

Huh? Must be some kind of bug with the display. I spent so long walking around down there, but it's as if only a few minutes have passed in this world. Then again, I heard that dungeons had a strange way of bending space and time while they're still forming. Perhaps that was just another aspect of that phenomenon.

In any case, I was glad that my escape didn't involve getting questioned by the police or finding myself before a panel of government officials.

"Phew... I made it out alive," I mumbled to myself.

Looking back, I could see that the dungeon entrance I had just left was now connected to a completely different passageway. The door no longer led directly to the dragon's lair, but to a tunnel that looked more like the one I entered when I first ventured inside.

Well, at least the door doesn't permanently open right on top of that dragon. I guess now all this is settled though.

"Wha-aah?!" My own stupid wail interrupted my thoughts as Kessie floated past me. "Wh-what?! Why are *you* here?!"

"What *is* this place?!" Kessie asked. "Where are we?! What's going on?!?!"

"What do you mean *where*...? This is Hokkaido, Omori City..."

"*Hoe-kay-dough?! Oh-morry?!* What in the world, where in the world?! The Kingdom of *Hoe-kay-dough*?! Maybe the Empire of *Hoe-kay-dough*?!"

"Uh... You really don't know anything about this place?" I asked.

"Not the faintest clue! What's going on?! Is this another world?! What happened to the dungeon?!" As Kessie cried in confusion, I heard the siren of a patrol car in the distance.

"Shoot. Someone's reported this dungeon to the police! Let's run before they get here!" I urged her.

"What, what?! Who are we running from?!"

"Just come on! They'll turn you into something way worse than salted fairy skewers if they find you!"

She's the first intelligent monster the world's ever discovered, I mean! She'd be turned into a test subject!

"What do you mean?! What could possibly be worse than that?!" she whined.

"Just run, I mean it! Let's go!"

CHAPTER 3
PLEASE PAY ME IN YEN, NOT IN GOLD COINS

1

I RETURNED TO MY RENTED APARTMENT—THE VERY one I only just signed the lease on. Compared to Tokyo, it was unbelievably cheap to live out in the Hokkaido countryside, so my new place was much nicer and more spacious than the old one.

One of the few actual highlights of getting transferred was picking out this apartment, I guess.

"Hey what's going on?! What is this place?!" My new little roommate, impressively loud despite the tiny amount of space she took up, fluttered around my room. She eyed all the boxes I hadn't had time to unpack yet.

"What do you mean what?" I asked. "It is what it is."

"I don't get it! I don't understand at all!" Kessie whined. "What *is* this world?! *Where* is this world?!"

"Earth. We're on planet Earth."

"*Erfh?!* Where's the Continent of Emglasir?! The Holy Empire of Garma?! Or the Mystical Forest of the elves?!"

"Nothin' like that around here," I answered, pouring some hot water into one of the cups of instant ramen I recently stocked up on. "You want some?"

"What is that? Hot water?! What do you do after the water goes into the cup?!"

"Well, er... You're supposed to eat it."

"Ahhh, where am I? What happened to my home forest...? Where did it disappear to...?" Kessie sat sobbing on the wooden dining table in the middle of my living room, eating cold ramen noodles right from the cup.

She's so small, I bet those ramen noodles must seem like they stretch on forever to her. I don't think I'm going to have to worry about her food costing me much.

"So...you used to live in a completely different world from this one?" I asked.

"Yes indeed!" she answered. "I've never even heard of this place before! You have all these iron boxes running around wherever they please, right? This world is so gray and shoddy, I've never seen anything like it before!"

So...I guess dungeons really are *passages to some other world that this one happened to connect to four years ago. But what's the deal with that, anyway?* I thought, noisily slurping down my own noodles.

Over the past few years, people had gotten used to there being dungeons. *Even so, I don't think anyone in the world has ever met and had a conversation with an intelligent creature like this. I mean, maybe they've got one in America, and they're just hiding it...but that's just an urban legend. There are tons of conspiracy theories out there. If I'm really the first one though... Did I really stumble into two people—ahem— two talking monsters in one day? Not to mention I ended up taking one of them home with me.*

I wondered what that dragon was up to at the moment. *It sure looked like the dungeon finished generating since the entrance connected to somewhere new... Well, hey, I'm sure he's all right. I need to deliver those batteries to him sometime. Are we really going to meet up again someday?*

"Come to think of it..." I slurped down some more noodles and pulled over the treasure chest the white dragon gave me. "He said there were skills or something in here, right? Let's see what we've got."

"I'm sure they won't be *that* good," said Kessie. "The dragon didn't seem to care at all about what was inside that box, he just liked that it was shiny."

"Hey, don't be like that. The skills don't have to be good. I'm just happy I got something."

With one hand on my chopsticks, the other on the box—I opened it. I was met with a poof of white smoke, just like the one in the tale of Urashima Taro.

"Wah-pfh! What's this?!" I yelled.

Kessie coughed loudly. "Hey! I'm still eating! Stop doing weird stuff over there!"

Despite Kessie's noisy complaints, I heard a *ding!* sound—the same sound I remembered hearing when my stat screen first appeared. That very screen appeared before my eyes again, and this time, a [+1] was hovering near the skill button.

I guess this means I've got a new skill? That's easy to understand. This screen though... It sure looks like a Bapple BiPhone menu. I guess even in other worlds stat screens are designed for usability. They've definitely got their own Stede Jobs over there. Hey, maybe he reincarnated in their world? Ha ha, probably not.

With such idle thoughts floating through my head, I pushed the skill button, and the letters before my eyes collapsed, then reformed themselves into a completely new screen.

One skill... "Skillbook."

"Skillbook? Kessie, do you know what this does?"

"Nope, no idea! I've never even heard of it!" Starting to show a little interest for the first time, she came to peek over at my screen. "I guess it's a rare skill... Wait, you only have *one* skill...? Is that all? How in the world have you managed to live such an unskilled life?!"

"We don't *have* skills in this world, that's why."

I finished my noodles, opened my laptop, and opened a web browser to look some things up.

Humanity had gained three main resources from the dungeons: skills, magic, and a great variety of different things like ores and substances that didn't exist on Earth—including the monsters themselves.

When the first dungeon appeared, items found inside it were huge discoveries, overturning decades of humanity's scientific knowledge. However, as time passed, our procurement and research advanced considerably. Items were now ranked into different categories, ranging from worthless everyday items to those not even several billion yen could buy.

But like all resources, currencies, oil, and really anything worth anything, the value changes over time...

"...What's all this?" asked Kessie.

My laptop screen was filled with graphs of blue and red lines zigzagging up and down.

"It's Dungeon FX."

"I don't know *what* that's supposed to mean," she complained.

Along with the recent boom in virtual currencies, there were now plenty of charts that tracked relative values of different dungeon resources. This one was called Dungeon FX for short. *It's not even just for big investors anymore,* I thought. *Even regular citizens have started to focus their investments here.*

"Oh man, the value of that Blaze skill really dropped." Seeing how dramatically the value of that skill had fallen, I pulled up a news site—I figured something must've happened to trigger it.

Looks like a British adventurer discovered a skill that grants immunity to Blaze. Not like that would make this skill worth any less, but I suppose that caused people to sell. A temporary drop, I guess.

After checking several more charts and graphs, I sighed. "No sign of this Skillbook thing... Maybe that means it's undiscovered?"

Anyone possessing a stat screen was capable of handing over their skills to others by lining up their screens and dragging and dropping them across like files. *This site's divided into sections for sellers and buyers, and the prices are always shifting...but it doesn't look like anyone has ever sold a "Skillbook" skill online before.*

All I managed to dig up was a post from some online fiction website. There was a skill with the same name in a fantasy novel I found there. It looked like it was published a few years before the first dungeon appeared in New York City. *This guy's got some serious foresight. Well, not like it matters now.*

"Hey, so... Why don't you try using it?" asked Kessie. "Don't you want to see what it does?"

"I guess I could. All right..."

At her insistence, I activated my new skill.

"Skillbook!"

2

A THICK BOOK APPEARED IN THE AIR BEFORE ME AND fell to the floor of my apartment with a *thud*.

"I guess...this is what Skillbook does?" I wondered aloud.

"Hmm... It's like a skill that makes this book appear, then..." Kessie mused. "Or was that magic? *Maybe*."

I hesitantly reached down to pick up the book as Kessie watched from the air. The book seemed like a card binder, although when I flipped its pages, there were no cards slotted into any of the spaces for them.

"It's less a book of skills and more like an empty card binder... Man, this thing sure takes me back. I used to have one of these back when that card game *Yu-Gi-Ah* was all the rage."

"...Huh?" said Kessie. "Wait, stop! Go back to that last page for a second, will you?!"

"Huh?" When I did what she asked, I noticed there was a single card slotted into the page.

The card read "Blaze," and the burning fire in its card portrait made its effect clear enough. There were ten sparkling red gems lined up vertically to the right of the picture. Just like the trading card games I used to play as a child, the bottom half of the card was devoted to an explanation of the card's effects.

BLAZE
Rank E - Level 7 Required
Magical Attack
Deal 4 points fire damage to target.
Damage over time: 3 (burning)

"...What's up with this card?" I mumbled as I pulled it from its slot.

Immediately, there was a loud *vwhoosh* and a huge pillar of fire shot out of the book. Sparks began to fly as Blaze scattered around the room.

"Ahh!!!" I yelped. "Wh-what the heck is this thing?!"

"A skillbook... I see! So *that's* what it does!" cried Kessie.

I quickly put the card back in its slot and checked to see that my new place wasn't burning down. Luckily, the flames hadn't reached the walls or ceiling...but I did spill the soup from my cup ramen all over the floor.

"Skills are turned into cards, and that book stores them! And then the skills activate automatically when you take them out! That's why it's called a skillbook!"

"Hmm... I think I kinda get it, but...is that really all it does?" I asked.

"*All it does?!* What possible reason could you have to be disappointed in this amazing ability?!" yelled Kessie, excitedly flapping her wings. "It's really something, that skillbook!"

"But like, skills are things you can just buy and sell whenever you want, right?"

"Well, I think the way this works is... Skills you turn into cards with that book can be stored in there no matter what their level is. And you can have as many as you like... And it'll let you store and activate all the skills you want! Like, even the highest-level ones with the toughest requirements... Like the best magic ever! This thing's amazing, and totally not the kind of thing you see every day! It's *super* rare! Like, as rare as rare can be!" Kessie chirped.

"All right, I get what you're saying. You mean like, I pulled an ultra-rare from the dungeon gacha game, right?"

"I don't really know what you're saying, but... Yeah! That's right!" Kessie bounced this way and that in amazement.

So, well, if Kessie's guess about this item is right...
I did my best to organize my thoughts on the situation.

I knew that Blaze was the most common magic you could find out there on the market, and its consistent popularity and value has always been related to how easy it was to use. Skills and magic had level requirements to them, and they couldn't be acquired or successfully used at all without meeting those requirements. Blaze's required level was pretty low in that regard, enough that almost all humans older than children could pick it up. Essentially the moment someone got their adventuring license, they'd tend to go and buy Blaze. It's a skill they're bound to get eventually from some dungeon, of course—but a lot of people wanted at least one bit of combat magic that's versatile in a fight.

"Wow, so this is an awesome skill I've got my hands on. I wonder how much it'd sell for..." I mused.

"Huuuh?! You're going to sell it?! What a terrible waste!!!"

"But like, if it's really that rare... I could make a hundred million yen on this thing easy, right...?"

"Whaaaat?! This is why I detest you vulgar human beings! I cannot believe you would ever consider selling such a rare skill!"

I stared at the fairy as she protested, again considering how I could make a few billion yen or more if I sold *her* to the right buyer.

I gave in. "...I suppose you're right. I'm not going to sell it, at least not right away. It'd be pretty dangerous to let the world know I've got an item of this value, living in an apartment like this."

"So you'll sell it in the future?!" she whined.

"Well, once I've moved to a really high-security apartment, and I'm in a safe position to do the deal..."

"Wah! No, no! You absolutely can't!!! Kessie the fairy won't allow it!"

3

THE NEXT DAY FINALLY ARRIVED, AND AFTER ALL the confusion of the previous twenty-four hours, I finally got in touch with company headquarters.

"Ah... Yeah, we did hear about the Omori branch."

"Thanks, that saves me from explaining," I said.

My phone signal was as bad as ever, so I was calling from a pay phone conveniently located near my apartment. A branch of Showa Securities was now dungeonized—the morning news' coverage of the dungeon was already on the air, showing the building that just so happened to be swallowed up when the dungeon emerged from the ground.

"Ah, anyway... We're still working on a gameplan here at head-quarters, so stay home on standby for now."

"Understood," I said. "But I do intend to leave the company, so I would appreciate if that process could be moved along."

"Huh?"

"I'm sure I'm supposed to inform my superiors, but I don't currently know who they are..."

"Well, since the Omori situation...I suppose Uemura's still your boss."

"Well, it was his bullying that got me transferred out here in the first place. Since there's nowhere to be transferred *to* anymore, I think this is a good opportunity for me to leave the company."

"H-hold on a second. Bullying? Wh-what do you mean?"

"Please send me any documents you need me to sign for leaving, or training I need to look at for the next person who takes my position. Please pass my regards on to HR."

Click.

I hung up the receiver and left the phone booth.

Sure feels easy to quit a company when your workplace disappears. I had unfinished business there, but...I feel like working elsewhere is going to be more beneficial. I've got a good start now, after all.

I returned to my place to find Kessie watching TV, munching on a tiny, broken-off bit of cookie.

"Oh, hello! Welcome home!" she called to me.

"Hey. I'm back."

"What were you doing out there?"

"I quit my job. Or, I told the company I quit, at least," I explained.

"*Com-pah-nee?* Is that like a guild or something?"

"That's about the shape of it, yeah."

I sat cross-legged at the table, and Kessie licked at a grain of sugar stuck to her finger.

"You're okay with quitting then? You *are* going to have to support me for the time being, you know."

"It'll work itself out. I've got savings, and now I've got that incredibly valuable skill too." *Not like it seems like you're going to cost much either.*

Kessie didn't seem to be listening to my answer—her eyes were already glued to the commercials on TV again. At first, she was amazed at my smartphone, the TV, and even the vacuum cleaner, but she proved to be quite adaptable to her surroundings. After a day, she was already familiar with how everything worked and seemed pretty accepting of it all. She was already cackling her head off at the late-night *Night Talk!* show's *"I'm a Comedian, Get Me Out of This Dungeon"* segment.

"Ah! Look, look! Zukky-san!" Kessie started pulling on my shirt with all the strength of a fly.

A commercial for a well-known fast-food place was playing on TV.

"What's that thing?! I, like, *super* want to eat it up! It looks amazing!!!"

"Burgers, huh... They don't have those in your world?" I asked.

"We have something similar, but nothing that *big*! Oh wow, oh boy, oh my!"

"What are you even going to do with *that* at your size? There's no way you could finish one of those."

"I'll break it into little pieces, I can make it work! Hey, hey, let's go get one!!!"

And so we went out for burgers. Usually I'd leave the house with just my smartphone and wallet in my pockets, but that day, I wore a shoulder bag across my chest for Kessie to hide in... The little fairy insisted on coming with me, and I couldn't help feeling that she always *would* whenever I left the house.

"Whooaa! Amazing! What's this?! Magic? How does it work?"

"Those are just automatic doors..." I explained. "And hey, don't be so loud."

"You're the only one that can hear me, Zukky-san! Don't worry!"

"Really?"

We then lined up to order. There were posters up inside for new toys that came with the food—a set of characters based on dungeon monsters. Included in the options was a goblin toy, which made me feel a bit weird given my encounter with the real deal the previous day.

They just aren't that cute up close, y'know? It's hard to tell if they're old dudes or children at a glance, and their bodies have all those weird bumps, muscles, and veins.

"Hey, I never asked how it is you can speak Japanese, did I?"

"We fairies can't communicate physically like you humans can! It's a type of telepathy! It only sounds like your mother tongue, Zukky-san!"

"I see..."

I then realized how strange I must've looked, talking to myself in public, and took out my smartphone to pretend I was talking to someone on it. I resolved to buy some wireless earphones on the way home—not to listen to music or to call anyone, but to talk to Kessie while looking like I was on a hands-free call.

"Wait... Telepathy?" I asked as we stood in the busy lunch time order line. "You mean you can listen in to *everything* I'm thinking too? Or can you only hear what I say out loud?"

"I can hear *both*, you know? You're quite the straightforward person, aren't you Zukky-san?"

"Whoa, that's messed up. So if I think about something dirty, you'd hear it all?"

"Hmm... Well, if I decided to listen in, then I suppose so! I'm only really listening when we talk, though," Kessie explained.

"Got it. Well, I'll tell you when I'm thinking something dirty from now on, so don't go reading my mind on your own, okay?"

"I *do* know that you were totally staring at my butt when we first met down in the dungeon, Zukky-san."

"Yeah, right. Sorry about that," I said.

"*And* that you tried to sell me for a few billion yen. I know that too!!!" she cried.

"I said I'm sorry, okay? Look, I'll tell you from now on whenever I'm thinking about sex, or anything bad."

"That's kind of a problem in itself!!!"

As we'd been talking the line had moved, and it was almost our turn to order.

I overheard the man at the register to the left talking to the cashier. "What? Two thousand yen...? What is *that* supposed to mean?"

"Well, uh, your order comes to 2,000 yen..."

"Ah... Aha. I understand now, yes. You speak of currency. An exchange, yes?" The man plunged his hand into one of his coat pockets, pulled out a jingling handful of change, and spread it out on the counter. "Here, take as much as you like," he said.

The cashier began to stammer. "Er... I'm sorry, but..."

"What is it?"

"Do you have any Japanese yen...?"

"No, but this here is gold coin," the man said. "It should suffice, no?"

The cashier was stumped. "Well... Th-the thing is..."

What's going on? I peeked over at the pair—the man causing a scene at the register looked to be a foreigner. *Oh really? Their conversation sounded so fluent, I assumed he was Japanese.*

A tall white man with broad shoulders was talking to the cashier. He had to be 180cm at the very least. His black hair was combed back, and he wore a jet-black coat embroidered with gold. He almost looked like a noble from some far-off land.

Most Japanese people could never bring themselves to wear anything that edgy. Even so, he looks really good in that thing—you really gotta hand it to him.

There was a small girl standing next to him, looking concerned. She wasn't Japanese either, and her costume was mysterious as well—it looked like she was dressed as a priest-type character from a fantasy anime.

Maybe these two are anime nerds who came to Japan to cosplay? But why are they all the way out here in the sticks of Hokkaido?

"H-Heath!" she called out to him. "I-it's all right! Let's just go."

"No, Matilda. No. Hey, does gold have no value here? Why won't you accept this as payment?"

"I, well... I'm not quite sure what to say..." said the flustered cashier.

"We're hungry, you know..." the man continued. "We've been wandering for some time. This is a place where meals are sold, is it not? Look, take all the gold coin you like." I knew it wasn't my place, but I couldn't help but butt in. "Is something wrong...?"

The foreign man's tall frame turned toward me, and he looked me over. I realized he was quite handsome—like some Hollywood actor from abroad. *Maybe these two are here shooting a movie? That would explain the outfits.*

"Thank you for your assistance," he said. "What is your name?"

"It's Mizuki."

"I'm Heath. Would you mind lending me 2,000 yen?"

4

"MAN, YOU'VE BEEN A REAL HELP! SORRY ABOUT THIS, Mizuki!" said Heath as he ate his hamburger. He actually ordered a few different ones, as well as a large order of fries, juice, nuggets, a milkshake, and some ice cream.

That's a heck of a meal to be eating on someone else's dime.

After I paid for their food at the register, they invited me to sit with them as I waited for my own number to be called.

"This is rather delicious. The construction is crude, but the flavor profile is strong. I like it," said Heath.

"It's so tasty!" his companion Matilda happily chimed in.

"Hmph, I quite agr— Uhh?! What? There are *pickles* in this thing!" he complained.

"They accent the flavor! It adds to the deliciousness!"

"Well, I'd like them to consider that *some* people don't like pickles."

The two cosplaying foreigners continued their conversation, stuffing their faces with hamburgers and fries, washing them down with juice.

Heath... And the girl's called Matilda, I suppose. It feels like I'm watching one of those TV programs about foreigners visiting Japan— they've had a spike in popularity recently. But man, these two really are good at Japanese. I bet anyone could close their eyes and almost forget they aren't from around here.

"Oh, look," Matilda said. "It says they're called happy meals, Heath!"

"Happy meals! Ha ha, a fine name! A happy dish indeed. I approve!"

You two are the happy ones here.

"Are you here traveling?" I asked.

Heath brushed his hair back and continued chewing away. "Mm, that sounds about right. Yes."

"Why come to such a remote place?"

"Remote?"

"Well, I mean...why Hokkaido?" *Not just Hokkaido, but this Omori City is in the middle of nowhere. I'd feel awful for them if some package tour shipped them up here!*

"So this place is called Hokkaido..." Heath swallowed his hamburger and repeated the name to himself, raising an index finger in thought.

I glanced at the back of his hand and noticed his callused knuckles—he looked used to fistfights. *Be it boxing or karate, you don't get fists like those without thousands of jabs. He's definitely got some martial arts experience. In MMA terms, if he's about 180cm tall... Looks like he'd be ranked somewhere between a welterweight and middleweight.*

"Yeah, this is Hokkaido, I guess."

"I see. Hokkai-do," he repeated. "I like it. The systems your technology uses are completely alien, but you seem to have developed a highly advanced culture here. The population is a little lacking, but this does appear to be quite an extensive city."

I really have no idea what he's getting at.

"Is Hokkai-do a kingdom? An empire?" he asked.

"No... It's just Hokkaido, one word, not Hokkai Kingdom or anything." *Hey, don't go turning this place into some separatist state.*

"This '-do' you speak of—it refers to all countries? An autonomous region of some kind?" Heath appeared to be completely sincere.

Does he really not know anything...? Or is he just playing a prank on me, coming out with lines like these straight out of some anime? I've heard that people who are really into anime and learn all their Japanese from there can make some weird word choices, but...

"Okay, so you see, Japan is the country. Hokkaido's name just ends in '-do.'"

"Meaning, in short... This *nation* is named Japan, and this city is Hokkaido. Do I understand it?"

"That's right," I said. *Just how in the world did you even get here?*

This was getting to be more annoying than it was worth, and I started to wish they'd hurry up with my order. *If this guy wasn't a handsome foreigner, I'd just make up some excuse and sit over in the corner. Hell, I might've just run and not even bothered with the excuse.*

"Where is the individual that occupies the highest position in this country?" Heath then asked.

"I guess in Nagatacho in the Diet Building—the office of the prime minister."

"The city's name is Nagatacho then?" he asked.

"Well, actually Nagatacho's an area of Tokyo..." I explained.

"Tokyo... Is that the royal capital of this nation?"

Not the royal capital exactly, but I'll let that one slide. I can't sit here correcting everything he says.

Heath went on. "So that is where he lives, then... He with the highest position in the land. A king? Emperor?"

"Prime minister." *I guess it's like an emperor chosen by the people? I don't even know what I'm saying any more.*

"Prime minister, I see... Understood." Heath munched down on more fries. He brought a hand to his cheek and seemed to be thinking about something.

"Mmmm! The strong salt on these fries is delicious!" Matilda commented. "They're so good, Heath!"

"Yes, quite so, Matilda. This is a first-class world indeed. I wish Fiorenza could eat these too."

I watched the two of them talk. *They're too far apart in age to be dating or married but also too close to be father and daughter. With those different hair colors...could they be siblings or cousins?* Fearing another barrage of questions if I attempted to ask anything about their relationship, I stayed quiet.

After that, my food came, and I picked up the paper bag.

"Right then, this is it for me. Have a nice trip," I said.

"Ah, wait a second Mizuki," said Heath. "You helped us out. I want to thank you."

"Please, you don't need to."

"Don't be like that." Heath stuffed the rest of his hamburger in his mouth, stood up, and with a *vwhoosh,* made the stat screen appear before him.

"...Excuse me?" *He's...an adventurer?*

I was stunned, but Heath seemed to think it the most everyday of actions.

"Now take out your screen as well," he demanded.

"Eh...? But why?" I asked.

"Come now, there's no harm in it, is there?"

Wary of onlookers, I reluctantly displayed my own stat screen. The other people in the restaurant were starting to take notice of us—in particular, the masked high school girl sitting at the next table was staring at us intensely. Sure, it had been several years since dungeons started appearing, but it was still rare to see statted adventurers in the flesh.

Heath opened up his skills and began to navigate through the list, mulling over his options. He looked about as comfortable as one could be with the process—he was doing it as casually as someone would show me their phone.

"Hmm. Which should I choose?"

From what I could see, his skills didn't even fit on one screen. He started scrolling down, and the list seemed to go on forever.

"...Hm?" I blurted out. One of the skills in particular caught my eye.

SNATCH
Rank ? - Level ?? Required (Unique Skill)
• [?????]
????????????????????
• [?????]
????????????????????
• [?????]
????????????????????

It was the only skill in the list that was tagged in red. There were three related skills listed underneath it, but I wasn't able to see their names. *Is that a special skill or something? I wonder what it does.*

"Oh, I know. Here, take this. It's quite a useful one." He dragged a skill from his screen over to mine. There was a *ding!* sound, and the skill button on my screen now displayed a [+1].

"Eh? Huh? Wait, you mean it?" I stammered.

"Of course I do. I don't need it, so I'm giving it to you."

Wait a minute. This isn't like giving somebody a bag of potato chips... Skills are traded for hundreds of thousands of yen at a minimum?!

"Thanks, Mizuki," Heath said. "Let's meet again sometime. Oh, and lend me another 2,000 yen, would you?"

In the end, I gave Heath 10,000 yen and left.

"Who the heck was that guy, anyway?" *Some famous adventurer from overseas, maybe? I suppose he might be here to investigate the new dungeon. That was pretty fast...but it* would *explain some of the weird behavior and the incoherent questions he was asking me. With all those skills he had, the guy might even be world-famous! I'll look him up online when I get home. Heck, I didn't even know anyone on Earth had that many skills.*

The leading and best-known adventurer in Japan was a guy named Umaya Bara. I saw him a lot on TV specials and programs about dungeons, but I was pretty sure he only had about ten skills at most. *That Heath guy easily had over a hundred, but maybe his screen just works differently from mine, and he didn't really have that many?*

"Hey...Kessie? You've been quiet. Is something wrong?"

"No... It's nothing," she answered.

"It really throws me off when you're not chatting up a storm," I said.

"Ah, it's just..." Kessie stopped and popped her head out of my shoulder bag, looking a little embarrassed with herself. "That man was a bit scary, that's all..."

CHAPTER 4

'SUP GUYS! WELCOME BACK TO SHINOBU'S CHANNEL!!!

1

I LOOKED AROUND ONLINE, BUT THERE WASN'T ANY real information about Heath to be found. There was a Hollywood actor with that name at one point, but unfortunately that wasn't him. *I should've asked for his last name too, but searching "adventurer Heath" should have gotten me at least some hits, right?* I even tried searching in English, but I had no luck there either.

"So what was the skill he gave you, anyway?" asked Kessie.

"Oh, right. I forgot about that." I opened my stat screen and checked my skills. Below Skillbook, there was now another one. "'Chip Damage'...?"

"That sure sounds weak, doesn't it!" said Kessie.

"Guess I should look it up."

I went to Dungeon FX again to check the skill exchange rates and typed it into the search bar. My eyes opened wide when I saw the details and value.

"Chip Damage, Rank A... Lowest price on record...200,000 dollars?!" I read out loud.

"But how much is 200,000 dollars?!"

"Like...almost twenty million yen!"

"Whoa!" yelled Kessie. "Wait, I don't actually know what a yen is worth, so I still don't get it, but...this is amazing, isn't it?!"

"Amazing even doesn't do it justice! What's it do? What's this skill capable of...?"

CHIP DAMAGE
Rank A - Level 25 Required
Buff Skill
All your attacks deal 1 additional point of attack damage.
This additional damage cannot be prevented.

"Huh? That's it...?" I said.

"Zukky-san, there's more written on the screen. What does it say?"

Kessie couldn't read Japanese, so I read it aloud to her.

"Hm... 'Chip Damage. Valued extremely low at the time of its discovery, this skill's price has shot up rapidly in recent years due to a high number of armored monsters and ones with immunity to physical damage in lower levels of dungeons... Due to low supply, prices can range into...the hundreds of millions of yen'?!"

The explanation was much longer, but in summary... There are things called skill combos, where you combine skills to make them more effective. People have come up with all kinds of ideas for combos, but the centerpiece for a lot of them was the additional true damage from this Chip Damage skill. *I mean, it can't be a finisher all on its own, but when combined with other buff skills, it can produce explosive amounts of true damage...*

The skill was flexible too, useful for taking down monsters with special resistances that otherwise might be hard to beat. A well-known French adventurer first realized how useful it was and started using it in dungeons. *Famous adventurers sure can have serious effects on fluctuating prices.*

"Oh, it requires level 25... I'm still at 10."

"Why don't you try putting it in your skillbook?" asked Kessie.

"Oh, right. I wonder if it really does let me ignore level requirements?"

I activated Skillbook, imagining myself holding a book out in front of me. The thick card binder appeared above my hand. *It must've fallen on the floor the first time because I wasn't picturing it right.*

When I opened the book, there was a message displayed: *"One skill has not yet been carded. Card skill?"*

Wow, this really is a user-friendly interface. Even my old man could use this thing.

I went to press "Yes" on the display, but I stopped myself.

"What's wrong? Hurry up and turn it into a card!" Kessie yelled.

"Hold on, I was just thinking about something," I said. "Once I turn Chip Damage into a card, I might not be able to turn it back."

"Hmm... I wonder what will happen."

"Turning twenty million yen into a skill card is a bit..." I trailed off.

"But, but...Skillbook itself is worth loads of money, right? You still have *this*, even if things do get dicey!"

"I suppose you're right, but..." I groaned. "I could do all kinds of things with twenty million yen..."

I started flipping through the binder to see if anything else was written inside. I stopped on the page that Blaze was slotted into and took a closer look at the card itself.

"Huh? What are these?"

I could see strange symbols carved into the right side of the card. There were ten circular marks, nine of which were glowing red. Only the one right at the top was blacked out.

Were these always here? Maybe they were...but I don't think they were glowing, right? I thought it was just a part of the card design.

"Huh?" I started. "Could it be..."

"What is it?"

"Does this mean that Skillbook cards have a limited number of uses?!"

"Hmm? Oh, you're right. It looks like the maximum number of uses is ten, and one of them's used up," Kessie commented.

"Aha..."

So this Skillbook thing... There's no question that it's a powerful skill in and of itself, but there's still a lot I don't know about using it. For instance, I get that there's a limited number of Blaze uses, but what about Chip Damage? How does it work for ongoing effects? Would I get a set duration out of one use?

Eh, no sense in thinking about it now. I need to try out more skills.

As Kessie and I talked it over, the doorbell rang.

"Oh, who's that? Kessie, go hide somewhere."

"Roger that! I'm on it!"

I thought about who might be at the door as I walked over to it. *Someone from the office, maybe? A delivery?*

I looked through the peephole...to see a cute girl, perhaps a high schooler, sporting a neat black bob. She was wearing a white mask over her mouth, a hoodie, and had a backpack with her.

"...Huh?" *Who the heck's this girl? Does she have the wrong address or something?*

The girl was fidgeting a little and had both hands behind her back.

It looks like she's holding something...but what? As I turned the lock to open it, a terrible thought drifted into my mind. *Is this like... a honey trap or something? Like, somehow it got out that I have rare skills, or maybe she knows about Kessie...and the moment I open this door, some big tough guys are going to put a bag over my head and...!*

I hesitated, my hand frozen on the doorknob, but a moment later, it was yanked open from the other side with a *clunk*.

"Ah?!" *So it IS a honey trap? They've come for me?!* I felt cold sweat flooding the back of my neck, and I felt myself shying away from the door.

However, the moment the door opened, I heard a high-pitched voice. "Hey guys—! This is Himekawa Shinobu from Shinobu's channel—!"

The young girl barged right into my apartment, a video camera in hand.

"...Wh-whaa?!"

2

"**A**H. APOLOGIES FOR MY LACK OF AN APPOINTMENT. You're Mizuki Ryosuke-san, I take it?" She walked toward me with the little camera in her hand still rolling. In a 180-degree turn from her explosive entrance, her tone was suddenly calm and reasonable.

"Well, yes... But what do you want? What's going on?" I asked, a little frightened. *Why's this mysterious kid's mood bouncing up and down like a yo-yo?*

"Oh, the camera's on, but I'll censor your face later," she told me. "Please don't worry about that."

"That really isn't the problem here."

"...Wait, you mean I can do a face reveal?!"

"No, not that either! What are you saying? *Did you say Shinobu's Channel?*"

"Yes! I'm a YourTuber. My name's Himekawa Shinobu," she repeated. "Ah, just wait there a minute."

She then pointed the camera at herself and turned around so we were both in the shot.

"'Sup guys! Welcome to Shinobu's Channel! Today's part one of our dungeon clearing series! We're visiting the house of an *actual* adventurer! Yaaaay!"

"..."

"..."

A few seconds passed in complete silence. She then pointed the camera back in my direction.

"Right then," she said, all business again. "I've got two intro options there and a point I can cut at, so we're good."

"You're nothing like you are on camera!"

"Eh? So you aren't an adventurer, Mizuki-san?"

"Nope."

"Man... Seriously?"

She's kind of a downer at heart, huh... But she's the one who got herself all worked up just to get so disappointed in me—what am I supposed to say to that?

"And I spent alllll this time tailing you," she sighed. "I was thinking, OMG, there's actually an adventurer out here in the countryside, y'know?"

"Hey, you're the one who read that wrong. It's not on me." I told her to turn off the camera, and she clicked her tongue at me in response from her seat across the living room table.

Apparently, she saw me at the hamburger place at lunch when I was talking to Heath. When she watched me open my stat screen, she decided I must be an adventurer. Then, she followed me home and went back to get her recording gear once she knew my address.

"Even so, why did you need to burst in like that?" I said. "Do you want an interview or something?"

"I already told you! I'm a YourTuber." Shinobu took out a slim 11-inch laptop from her rucksack, quickly pushed some buttons, and turned the screen towards me. "I do *Shinobu's Channel*. Look."

"Right, right, I get it. You didn't actually need to show me."

"Please, look at the subscriber count."

"30,000 people, eh?"

"It's actually *32,400* people," she corrected me.

"What's the difference?"

She sighed at me. "You grown-ups are no good, and this is why. You won't even *attempt* to understand the size of this number... Just how big it really is, that extra 2,400 people."

Yeah? Well you're the one who stalked me and barged into my house without an appointment, kid. How come I'm the one getting lectured here?

"Are you even listening? A channel with 30,000 subscribers on YourTube can easily earn you more than the average monthly wage of a salaryman!"

"Right, okay, okay. You're quite the high schooler, I get it."

Making that much money at her age really is something. We're in an era where students can easily earn more before they graduate than people actually in the workforce just by uploading videos to social media. We're really living in an amazing world. If you told me all this back when I was in high school, I never would've believed you...!

Or any of that stuff about dungeons popping up all over the world, for that matter.

She started up again, pulling me from my thoughts. "Well, there was that dungeon that formed near here just recently, right?"

"Yeah."

"It's, like, super-hot news right now. I figured if I could get a video of someone exploring that thing, it could go viral!"

"So you came to ask me because you thought I was an adventurer?" I asked.

"Yep."

I was pretty sure there were some regulations about it, but if I remembered correctly, licensed adventurers could take people along with them into dungeons.

"I thought I could maybe get a video out of it. Like, a vlog exploring a new dungeon would definitely do numbers and get my sub count up! And once I got statted, I could get footage of that too."

"I know what you're thinking, and what you're saying..."

"Aren't you going to get an adventuring license?" she pressed. "I hear they're easy to get hold of once you've been statted."

"I'm already partway through the process," I said.

"For real?"

After I came back from the fast-food place, I did my application online. Once upon a time, there were strict regulations and tests for anyone wanting to become an adventurer, and it was on par with astronaut and pilot applications... But since the world had started to compete for dungeon resources, all kinds of systems were created to support adventurers. The government was happy to print licenses much more freely in an attempt to stimulate the economy.

But there are still some restrictions—you can't be unemployed or have less than a certain amount stored up in savings. It's likely their way of discouraging people from risking danger down in the dungeons in a last-ditch effort to get out of debt and turn their lives around. I mean, I sure feel unemployed right now, but I'm still a company man at heart.

"Wh-when will your certificate arrive?" Shinobu asked.

"I still need to go in for a few interviews, but it should come fairly soon," I said.

"When you become an adventurer, will you take me down with you?"

"Gonna have to say no to that."

"Whaa..." Her expression turned gloomy as well—she seemed to have a hundred different ways to be down. "But why?"

"I don't have any reason to help you."

"But I'll let you be an almost-regular guest on the channel!"

"I really don't want to be a guest on your channel." *And what do you mean almost-regular anyway? Not that I even want a regular spot.*

"Why not? Don't you want to be a popular YourTuber?"

"Look. You're seriously mistaken if you think all of humanity dreams about being YourTubers."

And right now, I've got a bunch of reasons to want secrecy. She'd be nothing but trouble to be around, and it'd be an unimaginably *bad idea to stand out and show up on her account.*

...I shouldn't have told her I was applying for an adventuring license in the first place, should I...

I began to regret letting that slip and silently wept for my true nature—a lonely grown-up who got carried away chatting to a high school girl.

"Right. Anyway, I understand why you're here now," I said.

"Won't you take me with you?" she pleaded.

"I can't. Go home before your parents start to worry."

"Ah, no! Please! Wait!" Shinobu took out a sticky note and pen, jotted down a few lines, and stuck the paper to the table.

"That's my phone number, Lain ID, Tmitter, and YourTube channel!"

"That's *way* too much information, that's what that is."

"Contact me if you change your mind, please," she said.

"I won't."

3

SHINOBU'S CHANNEL - 32,438 subscribers

"Shinobu Shows You the 10 Best Products of This Year!
    [Lazy Presentation]"

15,000 views, 1 day ago

"[Best Episode Ever] JK Walking in the Mountains Gets
    Invited to IRL S*x Meet-up lololol"

80,000 views, 3 days ago

"JK YourTuber's Room Tour - Gone Wrong?!"

12,000 views, 5 days ago

"Morning Routine of a JK YourTuber!"

90,000 views, 1 week ago

"I Ate All the Desserts from the Convenience Store!
    [Top 10]"

9,478 views, 1 week ago

That's about it, huh. Yep. That's pretty much all there is. I don't really have any comments or complaints about the content. I mean, she seems like she's trying her best, even if these are the results.

I decided to check out her most recent video. A few seconds of a dungeon touring company ad played before it started.

"'Sup guys! Welcome toooooo Shinobu's Channel!!! Today I'm gonna be reviewing my top purchases from this year! Y'know, the past twelve months sure were..."

I clicked off the video. It wasn't because it was boring or anything, but purely a factor of how little interest I had in her.

Well I guess this is just how YourTube is... What's she even doing making a top ten purchases of the year video now anyway? You sure you didn't just see someone else's and feel like copying the format?

"Right then, Kessie. I'm off to that adventuring license interview."

"Gotcha, ooookay!"

She lazily waved a hand at me from the living room table, looking at the TV. She was entranced, as always, eating crumbled up bits of Country Ba'am cookies from a little soy sauce dish and giggling at old variety shows I had recorded. She seemed to like the ones with Matsuyama Hitoshi the best.

"I don't think I'll be long," I said. "Make sure nobody finds you, okay?"

"It's fiiiiine! Ah! If you're going out, then...can you stop by the video rental store and pick up the complete *Try Not to Laugh* series for me?!"

"You've gotten way too used to living here," I complained. "You're already a damn prisoner of the physical world!"

I put the documents I needed in my leather bag and stepped outside. Omori was a city out in the countryside, but the area around my rented apartment at least had some stores and city hall nearby. For some strange reason, though, my interview wasn't being held at city hall but somewhere off across the city, too far away to walk.

I was stunned when I checked my phone for directions. The city, for its population, was much, much bigger than I expected. The isolated towns and residential areas were spread about far and wide, like electrons circling a nucleus—it was nothing like Tokyo.

Are all cities in Hokkaido like this? Do they really have to be so damn huge?

I walked over to my beloved car parked outside and saw a familiar girl standing next to it, playing with her phone.

"Ugh." The beginning of my inner dialogue slipped from my lips. *It's Shinobu, from yesterday...and from that video I was watching a second ago.*

She noticed I was coming down the stairs, and fidgeted with her phone, waiting. "Oh. What a coincidence, Mizuki-san."

"If this is *actually* a coincidence, it makes me wonder what it is you do all day."

Shinobu closed whatever she was doing on her phone and stuffed it in the pocket of her hoodie.

"What, have you been waiting for me all this time?" I asked.

"Of *course* not, what are you saying?" she countered. "I was only passing by and thought perhaps you might come out is all." She held up a plastic convenience store bag, showing it off.

Man, you're really going to hit me with the inexperienced high schooler conveniently waiting for her one-sided love interest to leave the house trope? Wait, I guess it's not just a trope—she actually is a high schooler. High school, huh...

I suddenly felt a wave of nostalgia washing over me, bringing back sentimental memories of my youth in years past.

"What do you want?" I asked her.

"I looked further and there aren't any working adventurers in Omori City after all," she sighed. "Well, of course there aren't, but still."

"I can't think why they'd come all the way up here to live in a city with no dungeon."

"Yes, that's what I mean. You're the only one, Mizuki-san."

I sighed. *She still hasn't given up.* "What about school?"

"I don't go that much. I can make a living off YourTube."

"That's not a good way to think about your education."

"I wouldn't *mind* going to school if you took me down into that dungeon."

"Don't underestimate grown-ups...and don't go taking the real world so lightly either."

I decided to ignore her. I got into my car, but Shinobu stuck out her elbow so the door wouldn't close.

"Okay, look. Could you at least let me take an interview video? Like how you got statted, your story, the dungeon, that sort of thing? I'll hide your face and name, don't worry."

"I haven't done anything worth you interviewing me about." *Well, that's a lie since I've got information the dungeon researchers of the world would trade an arm and a leg to get their remaining hands on. But if I'm giving that up, I want proper compensation and CIA-level protection!*

"Let go of the door. Go home. Then go to school."

"Then will you drive me back home?" she asked.

"Walk. You're still a kid, and I don't want to get put on a list."

"You're a grown-up, and a meanie, and a coward." She pulled herself away from the door, shoved both hands into her hoodie pockets, turned on her heel, and skulked away.

Why do all the women that pop into my life have to badmouth me so much?

4

I ARRIVED AT THE LOBBY OF THE OMORI CITY HALL'S Environmental Facilities Department Division Regional Hall, Sakuradai Regional Hall. The staff working at this building with an incredibly long name looked to be busy handling various inquiries about the new dungeon. In order to apply for an adventuring license, there was all kinds of paperwork to fill out—and I, like the majority of Japanese people, absolutely hated government paperwork.

It's not as if I'm taking shots at the civil servants at city hall here. I don't hate the place itself, just that I actually have to do all this stuff... I try and avoid it whenever possible. You understand how I feel, right? Are there people in this world who are actually buzzing with excitement to go to city hall? You know what? Maybe there are. Sorry, I don't mean to be rude.

This adventuring license, though... I really need it now, and I need it done right. This super-rare Skillbook I've gone and found is an amazingly valuable asset, a skill nobody's ever even seen before. It's an asset for my future—for the next step in my life... Pennies from heaven—rare skills from a dragon.

Setting aside whether I'd sell the thing or not—or even if I was dead-set on selling it—I'd first need to understand how to use it and what it did. And that's why I needed an adventuring license, so I could delve into the dungeons as a licensed adventurer. The best way to understand the skill was probably through lots of real experience using it. I couldn't imagine there was any other way to go about it.

Long story short, this is a pain in the neck, but I have to get through it. The returns are too great to ignore.

And so my interview began.

"When did you become statted?"

"Two days ago," I replied.

"Two days?"

"I was transferred to the Omori branch of the company I work at."

"Ah, I see. You must be from...Showa Securities, of course. May I see your bankbook?"

This guy's real by the book... I mean, he literally has an interview manual next to him that he's reading from.

The middle-aged civil servant continued his *by the book* interview directly from the book. He stared at the document I handed him, took off his glasses, and stared some more.

"You investment bankers sure make a lot," he remarked.

"Tough job, though. It used to come with a daily helping of harassment from the bosses."

"*Used* to?"

"Ah, excuse me. Forget I said anything."

After the interview, I went to go pick up the DVDs that Kessie asked for, changed my phone contract over to a SoftBant one, and headed for home. There were apparently several more steps involved with my adventuring license application, including more interviews and even more paperwork.

They also asked me for another document I didn't have on me, so I gave up on a speedy resolution to the ordeal. *I guess Omori City Hall is in turmoil over this sudden dungeon appearance. I hear civil servants all over the country are complaining about the insane new workloads that dungeon management has laid at their feet.*

I stopped at a supermarket on my way back, and bought enough food and drinks for a week, and sure enough...

Yep. There she is. I had a suspicion, but of course she's here.

The high school YourTuber Himekawa Shinobu was in my apartment parking lot with her camera rolling. She was wearing her mask and waiting for me, all dressed up and ready to livestream.

Getting followed around by a high school girl is supposed to be, like, the start of some heart-tingling romance in movies and manga, right? Here in the real world, it's just terrifying, plain and simple! It doesn't matter to me what she looks like or anything—she just scares me. I feel like I understand better the stress that women with stalkers must feel, or celebrities getting chased by the paparazzi. I bet I'd turn to drugs too if I had to feel like this every day.

I stayed in my car, and Shinobu knocked on my window, pointing her camera at me.

I pushed the switch to open my window and stuck my elbow out. "Look here, Shinobu. You're just scaring me now."

"Do you know about the three visits of courtesy? They say Oda Nobunaga visited Toyotomi Hideyoshi three times to get him to join."

She had the story completely wrong. "At least now I know you weren't lying about not attending school." *Not to mention that story's about superiors visiting people of lower standing, yeah?*

"Can we make this work somehow?" she pleaded. "I'll take some naughty selfies for you and send them over if you like?"

"Please stop trying to make me into a criminal." I sighed. "Just leave me alone, wait a while... A bunch of other adventurers are going to flood into town soon. I mean, there's a new dungeon now. Ask them once they get here."

"The video needs to be fresh. It's important!"

"Haste makes waste—that's an idiom too," I offered.

"That one doesn't apply in the online world. It's like I'm talking to a fossil!"

"Why are you so desperate to get a video out, anyway? Why don't you just make the same kind of stuff you always do?"

"You watched my videos?" she asked.

"Well, yeah."

Shinobu looked a bit happy to hear that. "I've put everything I've got into YourTube. I'm definitely going to make it work! Now's my big chance. If this dungeon exploration video goes viral, I could be a famous YourTuber in no time."

I looked her straight in the eyes, trying to get through to her. "I'm not trying to insult your dreams or plans for the future here, but I don't think you need to be in such a rush." *Man, those are some long eyelashes. She's got the double-eyelid idol thing going on too, making her eyes look bigger.* "I don't really get this stuff, but you're already doing more than fine, aren't you? Keep this up, graduate high school, and I don't know if you've thought about college after that, but...maybe that's when you can get serious about this YourTuber thing, yeah?"

"My school's full of idiots."

"*Everywhere's* full of idiots."

I meant that as a light-hearted response, but a shadow passed over Shinobu's face. *I guess there might be all kinds of things going on with her at school.*

"...You won't accept, no matter what?" she asked again.

"Look, this is all you're getting out of me," I told her. "If something happens, you can come to me for advice, okay? Now stop tailing me."

"..."

With that, it felt like our negotiations had come to their natural endpoint. I picked up my shopping bag from the passenger seat, got out of the car, and shut the door.

Shinobu stood in silence, video camera dangling from the cord around her neck. I couldn't see her expression, but the dark mood was palpable. I could have left her alone, ignored her, and gone up to my room, but something felt off about that.

"What's wrong? Why so quiet all of a sudden?" I asked.

"...It's *weird*," she muttered to herself. "I'm pretty cute, you know? I get quite a few donations when I livestream."

"Hey, people like what they like. You gotta look after your fans."

"I thought a JK like me could take down any grown-up... A one-hit knockout."

"The only people who can knock us out with one blow are cops and tax agents," I countered.

"It's weird... *You're* weird, Mizuki-san. You heard everything I said, didn't you? Why won't you accept?"

I paused. *There's something up with her. I should get back to my room before whatever this is gets any worse.*

But the moment the alarm bells started going off in the back of my head, Shinobu grabbed the zipper of her hoodie, and yanked it down. Below her hoodie...she was wearing nothing at all. No shirt—not even underwear. Her torso was completely naked under that hoodie.

From her neck to her belly button, Shinobu's pale skin was exposed to the Hokkaido air. The hoodie sat over her chest on both sides and none of the important parts came bursting out, but everything in between was fully on display. There were no extra pounds at all on the slender young woman's body.

The moment I realized what she did, my social defense instincts kicked in. I abandoned all my things to dash up the stairs and into my apartment—modern instincts that primitive man did not possess. Society trained us to protect our underage citizens, and the law gave us the instinct to run from them.

"Wh-what the hell are you doing?! Come on! Are you crazy or what?!" I yelled.

"Y-you're the c-crazy one! There's a beautiful girl standing right in front of you doing *this*, and you don't feel even a *teensy* bit of lust?! Are you impotent or something?! You don't feel *anything at all* down there?!"

"You're going about this the wrong way! Go back to school! Maybe they can hammer that twisted personality outta you!"

"Y-you! I-I'm going to curse you!" she cried back. "I hope all your luck with women disappears! That all your romances shrivel up and die! I hope you don't even *have* a marriage line on your palm!!!"

"Shut up, you goddamn pervert! Stop trying to involve me in all this! Go back to YourTube! Go! Live your own life already!" I yelled.

"I-I don't need you! I'll never ask you for anything again! It'll be too late to regret treating me like this once I'm a YourTubing national treasure! I can do all this on my own! You limp dick! I hope you stay floppy forever! I hope your time in the sun gets wiped out by some bug! I hope you're so unpopular it causes you problems in the real world!"

I ran up the steps to my apartment with her curses ringing in my ears. I unlocked the door and ran inside. I kicked off my shoes and stumbled exhausted into the living room to find Kessie watching TV in her usual spot.

"Ohoh? Welcome home!"

"Th-thanks..." I mumbled. "Good to be back."

"Did you get the DVDs I asked for?" she asked.

"Yeah... I did." But it was only then that I realized I left them in the car. "I'll give you them later."

"Really?! Thank you! I really want to see that *Try Not to Laugh at the Adventurer School* episode! Hey, Zukky-san, let's eat some cookies and watch it together, 'kay?"

Seeing Kessie so happy suddenly made me kind of want to cry. "You've always got your butt and your boobs out, but you're super nice compared to that crazy stalker pervert outside..."

"...Huh? Where did *that* come from? That was barely even a compliment! What?"

CHAPTER 5

UNAUTHORIZED OPERATION— PLEASE RELOAD CARD INTO CARD BINDER AND TRY AGAIN

1

AFTER SEVERAL MORE STEPS THROUGH THE BUREAU-cracy, my adventuring license and adventuring card were finally delivered to me. The card was about the size of a credit card and formatted much like a driver's license—but didn't look quite as lame. It was more like a credit card with a picture on it and satisfied my desire for cool things.

I think some famous designer worked on this card, right? I forget their name though. Whatever, it doesn't matter.

The thing looked so good that I almost didn't want to put it away in my wallet.

Kessie floated over and saw me staring at the license. "Zukky-san, Zukky-san."

"What?"

"You've got your license, but what are you going to do now?"

"Well, first I've gotta go give that dragon his batteries."

"Huh? You're *seriously* going to give him those?" The little fairy looked taken aback. "I'm just going to be honest; I never want to see that dragon again!!!"

"A promise is a promise, nothing I can do about that," I said. "He *did* give me this rare skill too."

There was a mountain of batteries on the living room table, ready for delivery. *That thing has a long lifespan, but even so, I might've gone too far here. The machine is going to break before he gets through all these batteries—not to mention I couldn't manage bringing all of these in one trip. I wish I had a convenient skill for carrying things... But hey, I suppose I don't* actually *need to give him all of these at once.*

"Oh, and...what are *you* going to do now?" I asked Kessie.

"Ah... Well, that's a good question..."

"You want to go back to your old world, don't you?"

"I suppose I do, yeah...but I already half gave up on that."

"Why so soon?" I asked. "That dragon might know something about getting you back there if we go ask him. Let's give it a shot."

Kessie hummed in thought and folded her arms. She then made a face like she suddenly realized something. "But what about you, Zukky-san?"

"Eh? What *about* me?"

"What are you planning on doing next? You've gone and quit your job now, haven't you?"

"Oh, you want to know my plans for the future?" I asked.

"Yep, yep!"

"Uh... I'm going to do a bit more research into adventurers, and this skill I've got... Then, when I'm in a safe position to do so, I'll sell everything I've got and use the capital to become a full-time trader." *Once some proper money comes in, there are some things I've really got to take care of, after all.*

"I think that's a waste of the skills, you know?" said Kessie.

"Hey, don't be like that. Anyway, there's a lot I need to study and prepare first, but let's go down to that dungeon again once I'm done, eh?"

I opened my laptop and looked out the window. It was dark— night had fallen over Omori City. I figured that a night of drinking, looking up stuff about adventuring, and watching *Try Not to Laugh* with Kessie awaited me.

A note caught my eye, moved from its place by the battery mountain. It was the one that high school YourTuber Shinobu left when she barged into my apartment—a concentrated dose of TMI.

"I wonder how she's doing."

I hadn't seen her at all since our dramatic fight—if you could call it that—out in the parking lot.

Shinobu did say she was going to do all this on her own... I sure hope she hasn't done anything reckless.

It was kind of on my mind, so I opened up YourTube and searched for her channel name.

It's just her name, right? Shinobu's Channel. Typing that into the search bar brought me to her channel page—the same one I saw before.

"Hm?" *40,000 subscribers now? She used to be just over 30,000. That's a heck of a jump. I know she said 30,000 brought in the average wage of a salaryman, so I guess 40,000 must net her hundreds of thousands of yen a month. I don't really know much about the world of online advertising, but that's quite an achievement. Her personality aside, with that much initiative and grit, there are all kinds of ways she'll be able to make it as an adult. Maybe these are the kinds of kids the future belongs to now.*

There was a big livestream window pinned at the top of the channel page—but it took me a few times reading through it to believe the broadcast's title.

"Huh?"

My fingers moved on instinct—I clicked on the livestream, and the familiar YourTube video display opened on my screen. The footage was terribly shaky. I saw Shinobu wearing her mask and looking excited as ever.

"H-hey! R-right now, see! We're in a dungeon! We're diving into a dungeon!" Her voice was shaking just about as much as the camera was. The livestream was titled: *JK Tries Diving into a New Dungeon! Live Broadcast!*

"I-I'm okay! It's okay! Ahem, permission, yes. I've got permission to film down here! Ah-ahh! Thank you so much for the donations!"

Her filming light illuminated the bare rock of the cave behind her.

"Zukky-san, isn't that...?"

"Y-yep..."

The livestream chat was moving fast.

¥1,300 ¥2,000 ¥500

20:03 mitimaru: No way a high schooler is allowed to film down there lol

20:03 Machiko: This is like totally a crime, isn't it?

20:03 Nanashi: Here comes the banhammer

20:04 one fully: Here's the part where she dies...

20:04 Itou Shin: She said she's allowed, of course she's allowed

20:04 Love Shrimp: Huh? She's cute...

20:04 Oriental TV Moving the Japanese Archipelago 1cm for Each Subscriber: Good luck!

20:04 shibaNeko: White knight believers, lol

20:04 Million Subscriber Challenge: Permission story doesn't sound legit

"She's *definitely* not allowed down there," I said—the same man who stumbled into a dungeon unlicensed, breaking the law, and almost died getting out.

I figured it would be hard for someone to take me seriously, considering my own criminal record in this area. Filming permission aside, it was illegal to enter a dungeon without a licensed adventurer accompanying you. There were exceptions in cases like saving a human's life, or other extenuating circumstances where it might be necessary. But a high school kid's YourTube livestream definitely didn't qualify, especially not alone.

"Waaaah! I don't really know what's going on there, but she really messed up, didn't she?!" said Kessie.

"Messing up in the present tense... That idiot..." I muttered under my breath, holding my head in my hands.

"I-it's okay!" came Shinobu's voice from the stream. *"I'm still just at the entrance! Right at the start! O-oh wow! Actually being down in a dungeon sure is scary!"* The livestream's picture continued to tremble.

"Wh-whoa! Thank you so much for the donations! Ah, it's fine! It looks like the signal still reaches down here! I'll just be going a little further! I want to see what's further in!"

Hey, wait a second now, I called out in my mind, as the livestream kept going. *Stop. Leave it at that. You can still go back! Any further and you'll be even stupider than I was.*

"Hm-hm? I don't have permission? Criminal livestream? W-wow, there are some loud haters in here today!"

Shinobu addressed the comments as she went along—the adrenaline that was pumping hard through her system had her more excited than I'd seen her before.

"What? This'll make people mad? W-well, that's just fine with me!

You haters are nourishment, don't you forget it! You'll report me? Go right ahead, do whatever you want! Making people mad will only make me even more famous!" In her worked-up state, Shinobu sure was giving the naysayers plenty to work with.

All the blood's rushed to her head. She's too excited and not thinking straight.

With shaky steps, she continued into the dungeon, desperately trying to keep up with her chat as she went. She came to a fork in her path, and that seemed to be the limit of her phone signal. Static started to invade the livestream, and the audio fell out of sync.

"Ah-h##em! S-####so whi####ch way####should we go?! Let's star#t a poll in ch###at? Wh###at? My aud###io? Bad sig####nal may###be?" Shinobu seemed to be picking up on the issue. She positioned the camera to put herself and the two paths behind her in frame and continued to follow her chat. It was only then, in the darkness of the caves behind her, that something *moved*.

"Ah####so you ca###n barely hear an##ything? ###What? ##Behind m###? ###That's such a dead####meme, I'd###never fall for th####at one! ##Hah hah###."

Shinobu's laughter came through loud and clear, even over the static noise.

Suddenly, from the blackness behind her, a shape lunged towards the camera.

"Waah###ah###h###?!"

The camera rolled across the ground, and for a moment, I had no idea what was happening. Among the noise and Shinobu's high pitched screaming, came a low, ugly, growling sound.

"Go###b! ###Gob###!"

"Go###Gob! ###Gogo##Go-gob###b!"

"Ah###aahh###! ##Help!###N-no###! ###Help m#e####!!!"

There were scraping sounds coming through the noise, like she was grappling with something...and the camera on the ground captured it all. Shinobu was lying on the floor of the cave, surrounded by three short little shapes with green skin. One went for her legs, the other two her hands and throat.

"Help###! ###Waah##ah###ah#S-som-##someone###ah! ###Stop it##no##no#!"

She tried desperately to reach out for the camera—and then the signal cut out.

The livestream ended and her chat went ballistic.

¥20,000 ¥5,000 ¥1,500 ¥1,000

20:06 Jibetter: I thought this was outrage bait, turns out it's just fake, huh

20:06 Kuroko's Tennis: Nice acting, seriously. Subbed.

20:06 Oriental TV Moving the Japanese Archipelago 1cm for Each Subscriber: Huh?!

20:06 MAGIC NIGHT: Nah, no way those things are fake, right?!

20:06 I <3 You: Is this for real?

20:06 Kenji: Lol some people are actually falling for this

20:06 Trying to Get To 1 Million Subs without Uploading Any Videos: Isn't this seriously screwed up?

20:07 Itou Shin: Should probably report this.

20:07 Sad TH: You guys are idiots for thinking this is real.

20:07 Atsumi Youichi: Some individuals in this chat appear to be accusing this livestream of fakery, but I believe it's probably genuine. This should be reported. What do those who claim this to be fake have as proof, in any case?

20:07 Annasui: tl;dr

I stood up, put on my jacket, and hurried outside. "Oh man! She's in serious trouble!"

"W-will we make it in time, Zukky-san?!"

"We're going to have to!"

2

"HOW'S THE LIVESTREAM LOOK?!" I ASKED KESSIE AS I started the engine of my beloved Celsiar. Kessie was keeping an eye on my phone as it sat in a stand on the dashboard.

She called back to me, just as loud as I was despite her tiny stature. "It's no use! There's no connection! She must've been taken further down into the dungeon!"

"Damn it!" I blew through a pedestrian crossing so fast that if the police saw me do it, they'd stop me immediately. I got back into the right lane on a road with no traffic, practically drifting around one of the corners.

"Ah, ahh! Wait a second! The livestream started up again!" yelled Kessie.

"Seriously?! Did she get away somehow?!"

"No! It looks like they're still dragging her off!"

"*What?*" For a moment, I couldn't think. "They're dragging her back up to the entrance?" I asked.

"Of course they aren't!"

"Then how's the signal getting through?"

Dungeons were like regular caves in some respects—there might be a signal close to the surface, but further in, you'd be out of the service area. *It's not like the phone company's got signal stations down there, so I suppose that makes sense. But if the livestream's up again... Does that mean something down there is giving off a signal? How?*

"I-I don't have a clue! What's this *signal* thing you keep harping on about anyway?!"

"Oh, forget it! No point wondering about that now! Lucky break for us though! Make sure you watch where they're taking her!"

"Roger that! I'm on it!"

"Don't let me down and I'll buy you a whole box set of *Thursday's Downtown*, I promise!"

"All right!" cheered Kessie.

There was a simple fence set up around the newly formed Omori City Dungeon to keep the public from wandering in. Soon, construction was to begin on a proper entrance and reception area to manage access for dungeon-clearing adventurers. The whole thing had come as a complete surprise to the city, but it was certainly a fortunate accident. Tourists would come to see the dungeon, the local area would flourish, and additional funds and subsidies would be available to them for the work.

That said, this was all pretty sudden, so this fence was a real rush job. As for the security guard...

"Zzz... Ghnnk..."

I couldn't tell if he was a city employee or just a part-timer hired for a few days' work, but the lookout was fast asleep inside his little prefab guard house, hand stuck to his cheek. I ignored him and went to the entrance—only to find an iron fence blocking my path.

The bars were too tightly packed together to squeeze through, but there was a little gap at the top. It looked like if I scaled the fence, I might be able to get in.

"Why'd I have to get so brave all of a sudden...?!"

I put my flashlight away, climbed up to the gap, and just barely managed to wriggle my way in and through to the dungeon itself. I succeeded in catching my hip on the gap between the fence and cave roof in the process and lost a bit of skin.

"Ouch!"

Taking a little flesh as payment, the bars let me through to the other side.

Why didn't they seal this damn place off properly?!

Flashlight in hand, I took off at a jog into the dungeon.

"Skillbook!"

The book appeared in my hand as I ran, along with a *ding!* notification. *"One skill has not yet been carded. Card skill?"*

Is this going to come up every time?!

"Ahh, I'm going with no on that one! Kessie! Which way do I go?!"

"Ahem, uhhh! Whhooaa!!!" Kessie flew beside me, holding my smartphone and keeping eyes on the livestream. Her face was bright red, like the thing weighed a ton.

Hey, this model was sold for its slim, lightweight design. Not bad! They should put that even fairies can carry it in their next ad copy!

"Right here! I think!"

"You *think*?!" I asked. "That's not good enough!"

"I'm trying my best here, relying on my radar! Ah—! Is this that signal thing again? It turned back off!"

As I ran following Kessie's instructions, I touched a finger to the Blaze card inside my skillbook. I wanted to be ready to take it out at a moment's notice.

I can't have those goblins jumping me in the dark, like they did to Shinobu. I could do without a hand-to-hand struggle with these ferocious monsters in total darkness, thank you very much.

"Ah! I can see the picture again! A little further! Just around this corner—!"

"Huh? Then isn't this..." *Isn't this path connected to the place I found Kessie getting roasted over the fire?*

"Is the livestream still going?!"

"Yes! Ah, it's not good! It's not good at all!" she cried. "Age restricted! It's about to get age restricted! Something wild is going to happen!!!"

"Kessie! Get in my pocket, and the phone too!"

"Roger that! All aboard!"

She dove into the pocket of my jeans, and I started to charge forward—and then realized something incredibly important.

I'm not hiding my face, am I... Damnit, I should've at least worn a mask. I always realize this stuff when it's too late.

"Stop! No! Noo!!!"

Shinobu's screams echoed through the cavern. Near the center I spotted her, half-naked with her clothes ripped to shreds. The three goblins crowded around her, pushing her down onto a rock.

I've seen those three before... Never thought I'd have to fight them again.

The goblins were so excited by holding down the stripped-down Shinobu that they didn't even notice when I walked in. Their green hands held down her thin arms and legs and were just getting ready to make some violent moves on her with their hips.

That ample-chested, big-butted maiden had foolishly stepped into the world of the dungeon that ran on survival of the fittest, and the three goblins were about to devour her.

Wait, wait. Look, I get you're all turned on right now, but stop it already. Seriously. Any further and we're in real trouble. Like, yeah, when it comes to YourTube's terms of service, but for all kinds of other reasons you gotta stop. The only places you see messed up livestreams like this are those insane foreign ones where they bill you for tens of thousands of yen the moment you sign up!

"Heeey! Hey!!! Guys!!!" I shouted out.

All three goblins stopped in their tracks, twitched, and looked over at me. They let go of Shinobu and picked up their spears and knapped stone swords from the ground.

"Gob?! Gob!"

"Gogob!"

I had no idea what the goblins were saying, but they were clearly incredibly upset as they stood there in front of their prey. Shinobu was behind them, her face puffy and stained with tears. She stared at me in terror. Her clothes were ripped and torn, exposing her well-developed figure for me to see, but she didn't seem to have any strength to cover up.

She weakly stretched out a hand towards me, desperately calling for help. "Uh, ngh, Waah... Mizuki...*shan*...!"

You idiot! Don't use my name! Your livestream's doing numbers right now!

A cold sweat formed on the back of my neck and one of the goblins leaped at me.

"Gob!"

"Damn it! Blaze!" I pulled the card from my skillbook and called its skill name as the goblin closed in, spear in hand. A tremendous flame burst from the book in my hands, and fire enveloped the goblin.

"Go-go-go-go! Bbhhuuh!"

All right! I think I'm getting the hang of this! It feels like I really can direct the magic that comes out of this skillbook, or I think so, anyway! When I activated Blaze in my room, it just kind of dispersed... That must have been because I didn't give it a direction!

"Zukky-san!" Kessie called from my pocket. "There's another one coming!"

This next one had a thick sword, swinging it around like a great mace as he charged at me.

In that moment, a doubt flooded my mind. *I know I can direct this magic...but how did I do it? Was it because I said the skill's name? Was it the way I held the card? Was it just because I thought about targeting him?*

"Zukky-saaan!" Kessie screamed, and I stopped thinking.

No time to test that now! Just do it all over again!

I kept my card out of its binder and held it toward the attacking goblin. I called its name aloud. "Blaze!"

Nothing happened.

"Huh?"

Beep! There was a warning sound, and red letters appeared in front of my eyes. *"Unauthorized operation—please reload card into card binder and try again."*

What?! That's how this works?!

"Gob!"

"Aaah!!!" I ducked back. I dodged the goblin's sword, but I rolled to the ground in the process. "Nngh! Damn it!"

I elbowed my way up, and opened my skillbook, which had closed in the fall. *This freaking thing! I need to put the card back inside and take it out every single time I want to use it?! Stupid! I feel like I could've figured that out if I gave it some thought! I mean, I did give it some thought, but I'm just not thinking straight right now!*

I tried to put the Blaze card back into the binder, but my hand was trembling so much I couldn't get it into the slot. The edges caught as I tried to force it in, only worsening my panic and making my hands shake more.

"Damn it! Get in there!"

As I fumbled with the card, the goblin and his sword charged once more.

"Gob!"

Oh man! I'm not going to make it!

3

THE GOBLIN RAISED HIS STONE SWORD; A GREAT blunt blade ready to smash me into the ground. I saw the deep green hue of his skin—everything slowed down for a moment, my senses heightened.

"Wahh!!!"

"Gob?!"

I kicked out towards the creature, landing a blow on its stomach. Its little muscular body bent in half, and it fell down backward.

There's no way I could beat this goblin in arm wrestling, but this is one advantage my body weight gives me.

In that moment, I realized exactly why boxing was divided up into seventeen weight classes. I half-pushed myself up off the ground in time to see the last of the goblins running straight for me. I finally got my Blaze card back in the binder and pulled it out again.

"Blaze!"

Flames erupted from the book and burned the goblin's upper body. He missed his target and ran past me instead. The sparks reached toward me, so I quickly put the Blaze card back in its binder—without any difficulty this time, I might add. I felt a little sense of accomplishment at pulling off that maneuver.

"Gobb!"

The goblin I kicked to the floor moments ago got back on his feet and ran towards me, sword in his hand. I immediately pulled a card from the binder again and called out its name.

"Blaze!"

Three goblins lay defeated in a little cavern of the dungeon.

"Haah... Haah, haah..."

I huffed and tried to calm my ragged breathing as I looked down at the three creatures I scorched with my Blaze card. All that remained now that the excitement and high of battle was over was the awful smell of burned meat and an empty, terrible aftertaste in the back of my mouth.

I thought back to my days in college, particularly that MMA circle tournament. *In sports, it doesn't matter if you win or lose—once it's over, you get to compliment and be complimented by your opponent. You can clear the air with a handshake once you're both out of the ring. Crossing fists with someone in a match can even lead to friendship. But this... This was a death match, a far cry from the sanitized and safely managed world of sports.*

As I returned Blaze to its slot in the binder, I confirmed that four of its uses were now gone and there were just six remaining.

Right—I used one in that test in my apartment, and then three in this battle.

I snapped the book shut and it disappeared automatically. After trying it in my room back at home, I noticed that the skillbook disappeared when I willed it away.

"Y-you did it, Zukky-san!"

"Yeah... Just barely though..."

I picked Shinobu's phone up from the floor. It had fallen upright between a couple of rocks and its screen was smashed up, looking like a spider's web. I stopped the livestream and walked over to her.

"This is awful..."

Shinobu was sitting up on the cavern's floor, hiding her chest. Her clothes had been torn to shreds, and the remains of her white underwear and who knows what else were scattered around her. Aside from the remaining bits of cloth at her ankles and chest where her clothes were ripped off, she was completely naked. Even so, I had no interest in the high school girl whatsoever. Instead, I felt a tightness in my throat, and even a little dizzy. It seemed that my nervous system was still overheating from the battle.

"C'mon, let's get you up," I said.

"Ah... O-okay..."

I took off my dark blue jacket and put it over her shoulders. Given her height, it did a good job of hiding her butt at least. Her thighs were another matter, but there wasn't much to be done about that.

I got a look at my own jacket from the back, and saw it was filthy from my fall earlier. It was torn in a few places too. *Darn. That was my favorite jacket.*

"Ah-umm..." Shinobu's voice sounded hoarse from screaming. She pulled at the sides of my jacket.

"What?"

"Wh-why... Why did you save me?" she squeaked out.

"Because you were being stupid, that's why." I walked on in front of her, leading her out of the dungeon.

"B-but, I mean..."

"It was all that idiocy that made you do this, yeah? No matter what would've happened to you down here, it's not on me," I said.

"Then why... Why...?"

"Well, this is just one of those things, see?" I quickly worked out an excuse in the back of my mind. "You're still just a stupid kid, one who can't even wipe her own ass," I said, without turning to look at her. "That's what you've gotta take from this. If you get it, then go home, apologize to your parents, and go back to school."

As we made our way back to the entrance, I heard a *ding!* and something popped up on my stat screen.

"You have reached level 19. Distribute ability points?"

Leveled up, huh? I already knew a bit about leveling and the ability point system, but I didn't have a plan yet. I was planning on spending some time studying up first, but all this weirdness happened instead. I had figured actually going back into a dungeon and leveling up would be something off in the future for me.

Well, whatever. I can think about this later.

Ignoring the "Yes" and "No" options, I swiped the stat screen away and it disappeared from view.

"Oh?"

Just before the screen vanished, I noticed a little [+1] by the skill menu. When I opened it up there was a new skill listed: "Goblin Assault."

I guess I picked that up in the confusion of that battle. How does that work? I need to do more research on this.

Passing the iron fence and stepping out into the fresh air, we found the dungeon's sole security guard still fast asleep. I could hear his phone vibrating in his pocket, probably with an incoming call.

I'm impressed that hasn't woken him up...and kinda wish I had that skill of his to fall into a deep sleep wherever he stands! The guy's so not cut out for security work. Either way, someone must've reported Shinobu's livestream, and the calls are already coming in. The police and others will be here soon—sweet dreams until then, I hope.

I sat Shinobu in the backseat of my car, started the engine, and sighed.

"Look, if we *do* get stopped, explain all this to the police, will you?" I asked.

"A-ah, oh. Of course..."

"Where do you live?"

"Over by Suzugaoka..." she mumbled.

"Oh right, yeah. Close. I'll drive you home."

"O-okay..."

I started to drive, following her directions.

"What are you going to do now?" I asked when we stopped at a red light.

"Now...? What do you mean?"

"That livestream. Illegal entry into a dungeon. That's what I mean."

"Oh, r-right... That." I saw Shinobu's reflection in my rear-view mirror—she held her head in her hands. "W-well, uhm... I never expected any of this to happen..."

"It doesn't change the fact it looked like you were bragging about committing a crime on that livestream."

"Ahem... It was just to spark a bit of buzz, all right? That's just the kind of video I wanted... I thought the police might tell me off, but everybody would forget about it after a while like they always do..."

"The internet would be going *crazy* right now if I hadn't been watching your stream."

"Ahh, what do I do now...?" she whined. "Do you think people would believe me if I said it was all just a joke...?"

"I don't know."

"...I'll put out an apology video and stay home..."

"I hope people online don't leak your personal info or try to mess with you. But hey, you're already in high school. You made the choice to do this. Fix it yourself."

"Right..."

"And don't tell people my name," I added.

"O-of course not... Uh... Mizuki-san?"

The light turned green, and I stepped on the gas. "What?"

"Mh... Can I at least have your phone number?"

"Why?"

"Well... If you don't want to give it me, that's okay too... Uhm..."

"..."

I wished I could've said no.

4

WHEN WE GOT TO SHINOBU'S HOUSE, THE FIRST thing I did was explain the situation to her parents. After she changed clothes and was no longer naked under the jacket, we all went to the police station to talk to the officers on duty there. After questioning and providing a simple written account of the events (I made sure to note that the dungeon security guard had been fast asleep, of course), we were asked to return for another interview the next day. It was the dead of night when it was all over, and they finally sent us home. I drove home completely exhausted.

"You seem tired, Zukky-san!"

"Yeah... And I've got a million things on my mind," I groaned. "I'm going to bed."

"Me too!"

"Actually...want to go get hamburgers?" I asked.

"Whoa! Great idea!!!"

It seemed like Kessie was exhausted as well, but we both needed a bite to eat. We stopped at a drive-through fast-food place by the highway, and got fries, a hamburger, and an orange juice. While we waited in the car for our order, I did a search online for information on my new skill.

GOBLIN ASSAULT
Rank D - Level 15 Required
Buff Skill
For 1 turn, all your melee range physical attacks deal
  +3 additional damage.

"One turn?" asked Kessie. She was perched on my shoulder and peering at my phone's screen.

"A turn is... Like, it's to do with how long the skill lasts."

Magic and buff skills seemed to have set durations and only lasted for so long. Duration was commonly measured in "turns," and each turn was about ten seconds long. *That being said, I won't know the exact timing until I try it out for myself. That's just what I remember reading online.*

Goblin Assault was worth a little under a million yen online. Next, I started reading the skill's reviews. Unlike Chip Damage, which lasted more or less indefinitely and dealt true damage, it seemed like Goblin Assault required a cooldown before being recast, as it was limited to one turn. The fact that its damage was limited to melee range was a factor in the low price, since that made it harder to deal damage in an efficient and versatile way. The reviews went *really* hard on the melee range limitation.

Even with that, this thing's worth almost a million yen! The rarity must bump up the price. I'm not really clear on how much power difference +3 damage will give me...but given I've only got 14 HP total right now, the damage from this buff skill could take me out in five hits. Wait—is this really all that good? Feels like a metal bat with a full swing straight to the head might be more powerful. But taking someone down, like actually killing them in five hits... That would usually take a small caliber weapon, I guess. Anyway, it looks like this skill's a rare drop from beating goblins.

As soon as the paper fast-food bag was in my hands, I drove straight home. I left the bag open on the passenger seat.

"Kessie, go ahead and eat some fries."

"It's okay! Let's eat together when we get home!" she yelled.

"Right." I sighed, not really knowing why. For whatever reason, I had a strange, uncomfortable feeling. "Sure, all right then."

When I got back to my apartment, I parked in the lot, picked up the bag with our food in it, and climbed the stairs. I fished my key out of the back pocket of my jeans as I went along.

I wonder how Shinobu got signal in that cave... Maybe all

dungeons work like that? I need to do some research on it, just like with everything else. It's all still so mysterious to me.

When I reached the second floor, a man I could've sworn I saw somewhere before was trying to get into the apartment next to mine. He was tall with swept-back black hair, wearing a long coat of black and gold. Before he went inside, he noticed me, and his sharp eyes opened wide.

"Mizuki! If it isn't Mizuki!"

"Ah, uh... Heath?"

It absolutely was the foreigner I met in the hamburger place the other day. He was standing in the doorway, looking at me.

"Whatever brings you here, Heath?"

"Come on, don't be so formal. We're buddies, right?" Heath said.

Are we? I guess he must think we're "brothers" or something—it's a bit of a foreign concept to me.

"It's only temporary, but I'm going to be living here a while," he continued. "Don't tell me... Do you live somewhere nearby?"

"Place right next to yours, yep."

"Oh, great! What a wonderfully happy coincidence!" He grinned and held his hand out towards me. "Looking forward to living here, neighbor."

"Y-yeah... Me too."

"Oh! And I need to give you back that 10,000 yen."

"Ah, don't worry about that." *You did give me a twenty-million-yen skill after all. I have to remember to ask him about that...*

"No, I can't let you. That money was such a help!" he said, shaking my hand. "If you're ever in trouble, just say the word. Even if the whole world turns against you—I'll come and rescue you!"

CHAPTER 6

ROYAL EXECUTIVE ARMS

1

ALLOW ME TO BRIEFLY EXPLAIN THE FATE OF Shinobu's Channel and the high school YourTuber. That problematic livestream of hers, which peaked at 40,000 concurrent viewers, ended up trending on Tmitter and other social media sites. I didn't really understand the significance of it all, but apparently that was a lot of viewers. Her subscriber count shot up for a brief period, but since her entire body was exposed live on stream by those goblins that ripped off her clothes, her channel was terminated.

Debate raged online for a time between experts and the public as to whether the footage itself was real or some kind of hoax. It wasn't clear which side was pulling ahead, but several days after the incident, Shinobu uploaded an apology video to a new account and put the debate to rest.

In short, she stated that the livestream was genuine. She explained that the police got involved as well, and she was suspended from school as a result. She apologized for her reckless actions and promised to do better in future. Internet sleuths found and shared the name of Himekawa Shinobu's high school, her home address, and things about her family. They also revealed that "Himekawa Shinobu" was the YourTuber nickname of one "Tanaka Shinobu." Her troublesome behavior was reported all across TV news, and commentators expressed regret at the unfortunate incident...all while showing plenty of close-ups of her shapely figure—which I realize is beside the point.

The video of Shinobu getting attacked by the goblins was, and continued to be, shared around and spread far and wide on foreign porn sites, and the recreated Shinobu's Channel reached 20,000 subscribers.

She's in a period of reflection after that apology video though. She hasn't uploaded anything since then. Oh, but there is one other thing...

"Whooaa! Zukky-san, you're famous!" Kessie cried, watching the video again.

"Yeah... I had a feeling this would happen..." I stared at the computer screen and sighed.

A mysterious adventurer who defeated three goblins... People on a few video sharing websites have been commenting on the way he (or rather, I) fought those monsters.

The signal was so bad down in the dungeon that the livestream VOD was basically reduced to blocky pixels...but there were still tons of comments about the mysterious skill I used, and about Blaze.

Yongor334 5 hours ago
01:05 I think she's saying "Izumi-san." Could be "Mizuki"
👍 13 👎 0
Display 2 replies ⌄

Great Emperor What the Heck 5 hours ago

Goblins are way too freakin' ripped

👍 6 👎 2

Elmo [Trying to get to 20,000 subs] 3 hours ago

01:17 He misses once and totally panics lol

👍 4 👎 1

Display 4 replies ⌄

Oriental TV Moving the Japanese Archipelago 1cm for Each Subscriber 5 hours ago

This dude was awesome!!!!!1

👍 0 👎 4

"...Hmm..." I groaned, gazing at the comments.

Thankfully, my visit to the police station after the incident didn't result in a scolding. If anything, they seemed grateful to me for making sure the injuries Shinobu suffered weren't any more serious. If anything worse ended up happening to her, there would've been blame up and down the chain of dungeon-related agencies, and the police would've had to accept their share of the responsibility too.

And fortunately for me, they didn't pry into where I got my rare skill from. To them, what mattered was that there were extenuating circumstances to my entering the dungeon, that city hall had done an awful job of blocking it off, and that Shinobu herself was truly in danger. The skills I used to save her just weren't important to the case.

Luckily, the police stopped information about my identity getting out, so nobody has been able to pin me down online... This "mysterious adventurer rescues JK YourTuber" hype really isn't helping me though.

I hope it fades away and everyone just forgets about it...but I wonder if it really will?

Inappropriate as I knew it was, I personally couldn't wait for the next big incident to happen (not that I cared much what that entailed), and for all the attention to shift there, leaving Shinobu and the tale of the mysterious adventurer to be forgotten.

"You're a *celebrity* but you don't seem that happy about it, do you?" asked Kessie.

"What's there to be happy about? If my address gets leaked or something, it's only going to be more trouble."

"Cross that bridge when you come to it! You should be proud, hold your head up high!"

"The higher I hold my head up, the faster *you'll* be off to some research facility."

Well, no sense worrying about this now anyway. Who knows how it'll turn out?

I pulled up another site from my bookmarks, to check out more about leveling and ability points.

I leveled up in the fight against the goblins, but figuring out how to spend my ability points was tough. *What exactly is a level, anyway? The true nature of the concept still isn't really understood, at least far as I can see online.*

One theory was that levels and ability points were calculated based on the average abilities of all statted human beings at any given time. Levels ranged from 1 to 100, and it was speculated that ability points ranged from 1 to 100 as well. If a hundred people were statted all at once, the levels they found themselves at might be considered a kind of relative power ranking of their general abilities.

It sounds like levels are unstable when a dungeon is forming too, and you can level up or down without even doing anything during the formation phase. Apparently stats used to fluctuate a lot more too, back when the pool of statted people was smaller... Now, there are so many adventurers and non-adventurers who've undergone the process that the law of large numbers has taken the wheel and levels don't shift much anymore.

"There was a big level shift right before I went into that dungeon for the first time," I said.

"Really?"

America used to be the only nation in the world to have a Level 100 adventurer. His name's Wallace Chandler, a U.S. government agent and former Navy SEAL officer. I heard that he was also a genius, graduating from Oxford University with a degree in criminology. Since he left the military, he has been working as a CIA agent. He was the one who led the investigation of the "NY Dungeon," the first one to appear in this world, and he was assigned Level 100 the moment he stepped inside. They said that all of his ability scores were in the 80s and 90s back then too.

Four years later, he was still the only one to reach Level 100, earning him praise as the most capable individual humanity had to offer, at least according to the dungeon's standards. However, Chandler's level had suddenly fallen to 63, and adventurers across the world experienced similar drops, seemingly overnight and completely without warning.

Meaning...

"Someone was statted who's way, *way* more talented than Chandler. Well, either that, or someone's found a way to power-level and get their stats and abilities up insanely quickly."

"Huuuh..."

"And whoever this mystery person is, they're so talented that it completely skewed the level scale and knocked everyone else down," I said. "If Chandler dropped from Level 100 to 63, then the difference between that and 100 is the gap there—the power level difference between them."

With the prestige of the USA on his back, I hear their government has been searching far and wide for buffs and rare skills to keep the Level 100 top spot from going to any other nations. Those are just rust rumors, yeah, but believable ones. He's supported by the whole might of the USA, but there's still so much distance between him and that new Level 100 adventurer. Just who is this new guy?

"This is all a bit difficult... I don't get it!" said Kessie. "Are you sure about all this?"

"They're just rumors," I said. "Some people think our whole theory of the leveling system's wrong, and others figure maybe a huge animal or something got statted and is messing with the rankings... There's a lot of talk."

"I see... I suppose if a gorilla got statted, its strength value sure would spike!"

"Exactly, yeah. Or maybe a super bugged skill's been discovered or something?"

There was a knock at the door just then.

"Wonder who that is."

I went to answer it, and Kessie naturally hid herself away as she always did. *She really understands the position she's in here in this world, huh. Why would anyone knock, though? I've got a doorbell, use it!*

The moment I opened the door, I had my answer—Heath was standing there, his black hair swept back as always.

"Hey, Mizuki. Sorry to barge in."

"Oh, Heath. What's the matter?"

"I bought one of those computer things, but I don't really know how it works. Could you show me how to use it?"

2

I SAW THAT THERE WAS ALMOST NOTHING IN HEATH'S apartment when I stepped inside. His living room was bleak and empty, except for an open cardboard box right in the middle.

"This is the thing. I figured maybe you'd know how it works."

"Uhm, so... You aren't sure how to set it up?"

"I don't know *anything*," Heath said.

"Anything?"

"Apparently these computer things are must-haves in this world, so that's why I bought one. I got it at that big store down the road, Yanada Denki."

"Have you ever touched a computer before?" I asked.

"Of course not. Never," said Heath, sounding strangely proud of the fact.

I wish I could declare my ignorance with that much confidence.

"The merchant did offer us this 'Super Speedy Start-up' service when we bought it..." came a voice from elsewhere. It was Matilda, the same girl I'd seen with Heath in the fast-food place. She walked out of the kitchen wearing an apron, clearly in the middle of cooking something.

"Then, this one said, 'No, it's fine!' and told the merchant he would work it out when he got home. See?" she continued.

"I thought I could do it, but it's harder than I thought."

As I listened to the two of them talk, I peeked inside the cardboard box. Inside was a huge, insanely expensive PC, made right here in Japan.

Looks like they just bought whatever the salesman recommended to them. This is one of those machines you see all the time in big consumer-electronic shops—expensive as hell and loaded with bloatware nobody actually needs. But hey, Heath really does seem to not know anything about computers. Lucky break for whoever sold him this thing.

"Where would you like me to put it?" I asked.

"Around here." Heath pointed to an unoccupied space on the living room floor.

"...On the floor?"

"On the floor."

"Don't you have a table, a desk, or...anything of that nature?"

"I told you to cut it out with the formalities."

"No desk?" I asked again.

"Nope. Do I need one?"

"Well you don't need one, but it's going to be *really* hard to use this on the floor."

"Right. I'll go buy one tomorrow."

He's seriously never touched a computer in his life before, huh. It's like, he doesn't even seem to understand the concept. I'm surprised people like him still exist... It's like meeting a primitive man or something. Even remote tribes in Africa have smartphones now. This guy seems so capable and put-together that I wonder where he grew up... Is he seriously royalty from some faraway country?

I connected all the cords to his brand-name computer that looked like it could easily have run him 200,000 yen and set it up on the floor. Heath sat beside me, excitedly watching me work.

He really doesn't seem to know what he's doing here, so I'll set up the operating system as well. I mean, he did give me that super-valuable skill just for paying his check at a fast-food joint. I've gotta show him some kindness in return.

Heath gave me a round of applause when he saw the set up was finished. "Oh wow, thanks!" he said. "You've been a real help."

"It's fine, this is nothing," I insisted. "You *did* give me a hell of a gift."

"You must know so much about computers!"

"That's not much of a compliment, but yeah."

Heath opened up his stat screen. "I need to thank you. Here, take another skill."

"No, I can't do that. I'd feel bad for always taking from you." *That said, there is something I need to ask.* "So, are you an adventurer, Heath?"

"I'm not, no. Why do you ask?"

"You had such a valuable skill... What do you do?"

"I don't really *do* anything particular." He then seemed to think of something and smiled at me. "If I had to say, I suppose I'm an outcast of sorts."

"He really is a weird guy," I mumbled, staring at the website's list of skills and levels.

"Heath, you mean?"

"Yeah. I was going to teach him how to use his PC, but he said he could work out the rest on his own."

"D'ya think he can?" Kessie asked.

"Not really, no," I answered.

Well, at least I've decided one thing. Keeping the website open before me, I called up my stat screen, and finally clicked "Yes" on the level-up display.

"Oh? Finally chose where to spend your ability points?"

"Yeah. I'm putting everything into Stamina," I said, pushing the appropriate buttons.

"Why not into, like, *Wisdom* or something? Wouldn't that be better?"

"I did a lot of research... That stat doesn't actually make you any smarter, apparently."

I realized pretty quickly that stat points didn't necessarily give you exactly what they said on the tin. Wisdom didn't actually raise your IQ, and putting all your points into Charm wouldn't make you a supermodel. The system was actually that each stat had a certain set of skills associated with it. Magic Skills in general depended on Wisdom—how fast and how long their effects lasted depended on that stat, and getting it high enough reduced the rate of rare-skill misfires.

The original stats each person got assigned, however—those apparently showed their true abilities as a person. The Wisdom stat someone gets upon first entering a dungeon was their actual "wisdom," in that sense, and raising the stat higher through leveling up doesn't actually make them any wiser.

So what did all this mean in practice? The amount an adventurer leveled up past their original stat lines is like a boost to them whenever they use their skills.

Take someone with a base Strength of 15, for instance. If they level up and put all their points into Strength, they'll have an ability point score of 50. With that addition, they'd be at 15 plus 35 strength. Their initial Strength of 15 didn't change at all, but they get a bonus of 35 points when using Strength-based skills. Oh, but you can also go do actual physical training to increase your Strength skill, and that'd be reflected in your stats as well. It would increase your base ability value.

"So I looked a lot of things up, and apparently Stamina works a little differently," I went on.

ROYAL EXECUTIVE ARMS 133

"How so?" asked Kessie.

"Stamina's also connected to your HP, your life force within the dungeon."

"And?"

"The more points you've got, the more survivability you get down there if you ever get hurt or seriously injured."

I figured that one out after reading the account of a marine who was injured in the NY Dungeon while fighting monsters. The trained paramedic included in his unit believed the soldier would surely die before they could make it back up to the surface—but he didn't.

The additional points he had put into Stamina sustained his life, reducing the damage he took over time from blood loss. The flow of blood returned to normal the moment he left the dungeon, but ambulance crews managed to get him to a hospital in time and save his life. Since then, it became standard practice for working adventurers to put their points into Stamina if they were unsure how else to spend them. When I leveled up, I was given 3 points to spend. Putting them all into Stamina brought me up to 16 points there, and that increased my HP to 15.

This is the strategy for me—my life's the most important thing I've got.

A *ding!* interrupted my train of thought, and I saw a little pop-up in the bottom-right corner of my computer screen indicating I'd gotten an email.

From my old company, maybe? No, I don't recognize the address.

The sender was "Horinomiya Akihiro." I knew the name—but pigs would fly before the *real* Horinomiya Akihiro would email *me*. My doubts remaining, I opened the email and began to read.

3

ICE TO MEET YOU. MY NAME IS HORINOMIYA AKIHIRO.

I am writing to confirm that you, Mizuki Ryosuke-sama, were involved in the Shinobu's Channel incident—namely to ascertain whether or not you are the adventurer who rescued her.

Specialists claim that the skill you possess is not in their database, and that you are also not a working adventurer. I understand you to be quite the mysterious individual. It was indeed a surprise to see you in possession of such a rare skill in that video, given your unknown standing.

In pursuit of a certain goal, I have multiple adventurers currently in my employ. My goal has not been achieved, however, and three years have now passed with little progress made. However, when I saw you, Mizuki Ryosuke-sama, I was very taken by your irregular nature. I wish, if I may, to commission you for a special task, and if possible, I would like to speak with you.

Furthermore, I wish to assure you that I have no intention whatsoever of taking the rare skill which you possess by any foul play. I understand that such assurances in writing may do little to convince you, but I do hope you consider that if my intention was to take your skill, I would use much more swift and direct methods in obtaining it.

Thank you ever so much for your consideration.

Below the email's text was a phone number and a request to call.

My cover had been blown, and I figured there wasn't much else I could do but contact him. *But if he knows so much about me already, why not just call and tell me this himself instead of getting me to reply? I guess he wants to leave the decision up to me, even if I don't really have any other choice?*

"Sneaking around and sniffing me out like this... I don't like it."

I went to search for Horinomiya Akihiro online, and his name was quickly filled in by the auto-complete feature as I typed it. Next to the search bar was a Wilypedia article with some basic details about him.

> **Horinomiya Akihiro** (born July 12th 19X3), Japanese Businessman.
> Founder, CEO, and company president of Horimiya Group, Chairman of Dungeon Tech, and Director of Force. Largest shareholder in the Horimiya Group.

To be honest, I knew all that already. I may have quit recently, but I *was* an investment banker, and I could hardly forget the founder and current company president of one of the biggest corporations in Japan.

Never expected the guy to ever email me though... I suppose looking him up was just a reflex.

As a rule, when I didn't have anything more important to do, I never put off difficult tasks any longer than I needed to. Within a few minutes of receiving the email, I took out my phone and called the number listed. It rang twice, then someone picked up.

"This is Mizuki Ryosuke."

"Thank you for your quick reply. Horinomiya speaking."

"I understand that you'd like to speak with me?"

"I would, yes. But not over the phone, if possible. Could I invite you to dinner?"

This guy sounds way too humble to be the head of the biggest company in Japan...but I guess a lot of talented managers can be this way. I still can't discard the possibility that this is some elaborate plot to kidnap me and take my skills... Even if it's too elaborate, to be honest. But whether this Horinomiya Akihiro is actually telling the truth or not, there's still a chance that's all this is.

"I live quite far for a dinner to be feasible, I think," I replied.

"I am aware. I have taken the liberty of coming to you, as it so happens."

Huh?

I rushed outside, phone still pressed to my temple. There was an expensive black car parked in front of my apartment building—it seemed to have just pulled up. A driver in a suit stepped out of it and opened the door to the rear driver's-side door. Another man emerged, smartly placing one long leg before the other.

He doesn't even open the door to his own car?

The man was tall and slender, just past middle-aged, and wore a fitted light gray suit and a purple tie. There was a white hand-kerchief sticking out of his pocket. He looked up at me and our eyes met, phones still pressed to our ears.

He was just as handsome and rich in person as he was in the count-less financial newspaper and online news articles I read about him.

"It is nice to meet you, Mizuki Ryosuke-san. My name is Horinomiya Akihiro."

Oh boy.

4

RICH GUYS ARE ALWAYS USED TO RECEIVING A CERTAIN *level of service, wherever they go, huh. And this guy— Horinomiya Akihiro, CEO and head of Horimiya Group— is no exception.*

ROYAL EXECUTIVE ARMS 137

"Please, don't let this worry you," he said.

I sat across from him at the table, feeling a little uncomfortable already.

"As you can see, we are in a restaurant, nothing more. If anything should occur, you need only make your escape... And, well, as I expressed in my email, if I intended on hurting you, I would not trouble myself with revealing my face and name. I expect I would hire another individual for the purpose and take far more direct and effective measures—though of course I have no intention of doing anything of the sort."

There wasn't much I could say to that.

We were sitting in a restaurant along the highway, some way away from Omori City itself. It was a lonely place out in the countryside, but once we stepped inside, it was much nicer than I expected. There was none of the pushy service you might get at an expensive place in Tokyo, but the staff seemed reliable and good at their jobs. There was classical music playing at just the right volume, and the space felt quiet and dignified. Horinomiya had offered to take me there, but I followed behind his car in my Celsiar instead.

"The chef is an old friend," he said as we waited for our food, try- ing to break the ice. Two of his attendants were on hand, dressed all in black—one waited inside the restaurant, and one was stationed outside.

"He's very skilled at his work and used to run a top-notch estab- lishment in Tokyo. He moved to Hokkaido for the fresh air when his child became ill. They wished for somewhere quiet, I believe."

"I envy that he can work wherever in the world he chooses to," I said.

"It's quite an ideal way to live. I furnished him with some as- sistance when he began his venture here. Today, he has booked out this whole restaurant for us as thanks."

"So?" I said, interrupting the niceties. "What is it you want to ask of me?"

"I will give you an advance of ten million yen," he replied, not missing a beat. "400 million upon successful completion."

I was trying to take control of this conversation, but he's used to making deals.

I felt as if he'd taken the measure of some indistinguishable interval that existed over the negotiating table and swiftly tried to slip me into his confidence.

"I can offer you some compensation for simply listening to what I have to say. Will you agree to do so?"

"I'll take what I can get, yes."

Our starters arrived on fine white china. The food was arranged and sculpted to perfection like works of art, vivid and colorful.

Does this stuff actually taste good? I always wondered.

"My request is that you retrieve a certain item for me from the depths of a dungeon," he said.

"What is the item?"

"Do you know what a 'Blessing of Eir' is? Only one has ever been discovered."

"Yes," I said. "The item is quite well-known."

BLESSING OF EIR
Rank S - No Level Requirement
Magic Item
Fully restore all targets' HP and MP while healing all
    status effects. (One-time use.)

That thing's super rare... I think Wallace Chandler's the only one who ever found one, all the way down in the NY Dungeon.

"When the strongest adventurer in the world, Mr. Chandler, used the item on a seriously injured researcher accompanying him through the dungeon, it healed not only his wounds, but the throat cancer he was undergoing chemotherapy for," said Horinomiya. "I understand it's a famous story."

"That's the item you want, then?" I asked.

"It is indeed. I have spent three years searching for it."

"I'm sorry, I know this is rude of me to ask, but...is something ailing you?"

I never heard anything about the company president of Horimiya Group being sick. Maybe they kept it quiet so their stocks wouldn't plummet?

"I am not sick, no. Healthy as can be, in fact. I pay proper mind to building sound habits, after all." He smiled at me fearlessly. Even the wrinkles on his skin outlining the muscles of his face were clear and sharp. He was the very picture of health. "However," he continued, "nobody can be sure when disease will strike and come to take one's life away."

"So you're searching for this item to dispel your fears about the future?"

"Indeed, yes. The company which I have built, Horimiya Group, has already grown to be one of the leading companies in Japan. I have not been shy about expanding the business into a variety of different sectors, and I expect us to continue growing."

He seemed then to remember that the food had arrived and began to eat. He silently picked out a bright red shrimp with his fork, and delicately tasted it.

His expression clouded suddenly. "If I had one concern... It would be a concern for the time at which I, the manager of this whole affair, should hand over the reins. *That* is my only worry. Nobody can guide the Horimiya Group as safely and successfully as I am able to. I could search the whole world and never find a CEO as capable. Rarer than the rarest of dungeon items, perhaps."

"..."

"But this request of mine is not born of personal desire. I wish that the 80,000 employees of Horimiya Group should retain their secure employment, and the salaries to support their lives. Have I made myself understood?"

Oh man. This Horinomiya guy... He acts like a gentleman, but he's got a tongue for this self-serving, self-adoring crap. I wonder if this is just what happens when a guy gets that much power—do they all get stuck in these trains of thought?

"I understand," I said, trying to bring the exchange to a close. *But hey, I at least want a chance to eat some of this stuff.*

I picked up my fork and continued. "I don't believe I can be of much use to you. I only recently received my adventuring license, and I can still only dream of actually going down into the deeper parts of a real dungeon."

"I would not be asking you to go alone," said Horinomiya, wiping the corner of his mouth with a napkin. He signaled to one of his attendants. "I would like for you to accompany the elite adventurers in my employ and serve as their navigator on a dungeon clearing."

"Navigator?"

"Indeed. You are the only individual who has ever stepped foot inside the yet unexplored Omori Dungeon. All of my straightforward attempts at hiring adventurers have ended in failure. I am quite committed to this new dungeon, and especially determined to explore it... I believe that a wild card such as yourself might be just the ticket! That aspect makes you all the more appealing."

Horinomiya brought his fingers together in front of his face and stared at me intently. Behind him, his black-suited attendant opened the door to the restaurant's VIP room and several shapes emerged from it. They were a group of foreigners, perhaps American or European, each with stern expressions like soldiers. All of them were tall and broad-shouldered with their arm muscles bulging out from their short-sleeved shirts.

In their midst was a short, fair-skinned young girl who appeared to be their leader. Her long golden hair hung down her back, and she looked much like a medieval knight come to life. She wore an old-fashioned military helmet decorated with a golden eagle. Her armor was red and white.

"These individuals are the strongest adventurers that the United Kingdom has to offer: 'Royal Executive Arms,' or REA for short. I should like you to accompany them into this new unknown world! My wish is for you to clear the Omori Dungeon together!"

CHAPTER 7

ARE YOU SURE YOUR AUTO-TRANSLATE SKILL'S WORKING RIGHT?

1

"SO YOU'RE MIZUKI RYOSUKE?" ASKED THE YOUNG, golden-haired girl. She was dressed up as an ancient knight from the Middle Ages and her metal armor clinked with every step as she approached our table. The burly-looking soldiers trailed behind her.

"That's right, yes... You can speak Japanese?" I asked.

"The skill's name is Auto-Translate. You can hardly call yourself an adventurer without knowing at least that much," she said, looking down at me.

Atop her head she wore an imposing helmet decorated with a golden eagle, which looked more fitting for an old war general. It was like the one the Iron Chancellor Bismark wore in the history textbooks I read at school, with an iron spike sticking out from the top, garnished with a red feather.

"My name is Carol. Carol Middleton. I serve as captain of REA."

"You?" I asked. *I mean the getup sure is a spectacle, but she must still be a teenager... Late teens, maybe. Not an adult, that's for sure.*

"Is there a problem?" she demanded.

"No... Not really."

"Dungeon clearings rely on the level, skills, equipment, and experience of their party members. I am a woman, yes. I won't tolerate being underestimated because of that fact."

"Look, I'm sorry," I replied.

"Will you be the one guiding us through the upper layers of the Omori Dungeon?"

"Haven't decided yet," I said, turning back to Horinomiya.

He smiled and looked me dead in the eyes. "True, I have yet to hear your assent," he said calmly. "But, well... If your true identity, and the nature of your rare skill were to become public knowledge... that *would* be a problem, wouldn't it? It seems you're holding onto a grenade that might go off at any moment."

I glared at him. *You aren't going to use rough methods to get me on board, huh? Give me a freaking break. You never planned on giving me the right to refuse.*

It was decided that we would meet again the following day, so we went our separate ways for the time being. I got into my beloved Celsiar and drove back to my apartment, feeling like I was pressing my foot down a little heavier on the gas than usual. On the way I got a call—I picked it up on speaker, putting my phone into a holder on the dashboard.

"This is Carol. Is Auto-Translate working?"

"I didn't even know it was capable of *not* working. Yeah, I can hear you speaking Japanese."

"Sometimes it can malfunction over the phone. Is this your personal number, Mizuki Ryosuke?"

"Yeah. Did you get it from Horinomiya?" I asked.

"*I did. I will call you again, so ensure you save me as a contact. If you have any further worries or questions, call me at this number.*"

"Thanks for your concern."

The line went dead there. I didn't hang up—Carol just said what she had to say and dropped the call immediately when she was done.

Yeesh...

When I got back home, Kessie was floating up and down next to the door, waiting for me.

She must have gotten used to the sound of the engine and hearing my footsteps on the stairs... What is she, a dog?

"What happened to you, Zukky-san?" she asked. "Are you okay?"

"Big picture, no, I'm not okay. But essentially I'm all right."

"I saw you get taken away by that expensive black car—I was so worried about you! Did you cover for one of your underlings and give in to the mob's demands?! What was the settlement?!"

"What, even you fairies are into weird internet copypasta memes now?" I sighed.

Kessie landed on my shoulder, and I opened my laptop to start searching.

All right then... "REA."

Several search results appeared on the screen.

REA seemed to be a British party of adventurers, actually the most successful and powerful ones in British history. Most of them were rumored to be former special forces or had experience as elite operatives for mercenary groups. Then, their leader Carol went viral for a while online, even on Japanese websites, being hailed as the strongest, cutest British adventurer in the world.

I did a search for Carol Middleton herself, and a few tabloid gossip sites came up.

Carol Middleton's the strongest, cutest British adventurer in the world—but what's her *real* name? Does she have a *boyfriend*? How *tall* is she? How much does she *earn*? Age and work history summary!

Carol-san's super cute! So cute she's gotten over a million retmeets on Tmitter! Let's take a deep dive into who she is!

What's her real name? We think it's probably just Carol Middleton!

Does she have a boyfriend? As for her dating life... Sorry, we aren't sure!

How tall is she? Based on pictures, she's speculated to be around 150cm tall!

What's her net worth? She's the captain of the strongest adventuring party in Britain, so she has to be making hundreds of millions of yen a year, right?!

How old is she? Carol-san is... Sorry, but we aren't sure about that either! She's likely in her mid to late teens...maybe around sixteen years of age!

Where did she work before? As for that... Sorry, we can't say for sure! I'm sure she's got some amazing things on her resume though!

Well then, what did you think? That was the mysterious captain of the strongest adventuring party in Britain, Carol-san! Whatever she does next, we just can't look away, can we?

Man... These sites are such trash.

"I think that was a waste of my precious time, that's what I think!" Kessie exploded. "They don't know *anything* about Carol, do they?! Write that up at the top, damnit! Graah!!!"

"Calm down, Kessie! This happens all the time!"

In any case, it didn't look like there was any genuine information about her online.

Feeling like I reached a dead end in my internet search, the doorbell rang.

Fairies, YourTubers, influential businessmen... Just how many people plan on visiting me today?

Looking through the peephole, I saw Shinobu standing outside.

I opened the door with a *click.* "Well, if it isn't Shinobu. What's up?"

"Ah... Mizuki-san. Long time no see." She bowed to me. She was wearing her hoodie and had a paper bag in her hands. "Ahem... Here. To thank you for the other day..."

"Snacks? Hey, I think you're sort of starting to get this *manners* thing," I said casually, taking the bag from her hands.

There was a box of Hokkaido's famous "Shiroi Kataomoi" cookies inside. *Hey, I was meaning to get some of these. There's been so much going on since I got to Hokkaido, I just forgot.*

"I've wanted to try these for a while now. Thanks," I said.

"N-not at all... Ah, uhm... Down in the dungeon, I...I'm sorry for everything that happened."

"How've you been?" I asked.

"Ahh... It's been a mess, but I'm getting by," she said. "I caused so much outrage, but it does seem to have a surprising way of working itself out."

"It's not like anyone's going to come kill you or anything. At your age, you've still got your life, and now a good lesson for what comes next... Might even be a benefit to you in the long run. All depends on your perspective," I replied.

"Hah, well... Anyway. Th-thank you so much." Shinobu bowed to me again. She looked so meek now that it was hard to believe she was standing in my apartment parking lot hurling insults at me not all that long ago.

Maybe it's wishful thinking, but it does seem like she's matured a bit.

"Right then, thanks for these," I said again. "They're more than enough, don't worry about repaying me any more than this, okay?"

"Ah, hm..."

"What's up? Need anything else?" I asked.

"Ah... Well I-I..." Shinobu swallowed, took a deep breath, and looked into my eyes. "Will you go out with me?"

2

"**...H**UH?"

I sincerely had no idea what she was saying.

"I'm asking if you'll go out with me," she repeated.

"Go out with who?" I asked.

"*You*, Mizuki-san."

"Me and...?"

"Me and you," she said.

"You mean you want to date *me*?"

"How much clearer does it need to be?"

"Sometimes I need the clarification."

I straightened my back and tried to straighten out the situation in my head. *So... Himekawa Shinobu (AKA Tanaka Shinobu)—seventeen years old, YourTuber, high schooler—is confessing her love to me, Mizuki Ryosuke—twenty-six years old, unemployed.*

Right. Now I get it.

Looking at the situation from the outside helped me to slowly and calmly put all the pieces into place. *Logical thought really is mankind's greatest weapon.*

"So, where's the camera?" I asked, looking around.

"There's no camera."

"But that's what this is, yeah? You're clearly filming for a video."

"I'm not filming," she insisted.

"Come on, what's your title for this one? 'High School Girl Confesses to Unemployed Guy! Surprise Ending?!' I know what's happening here."

I was impressed with myself for noticing what was going on. *First time in my life anyone's ever tried to prank me like this.* I grinned to myself, a happy little sense of accomplishment washing over me at having seen through her scheme.

But Shinobu was just staring at me quietly from underneath her slightly uneven bangs. "...Now you're just hurting my feelings."

"Hmph. I didn't think you had any stage talent. But hey, not bad. You've got the looks for a daytime variety show, why don't you give acting a shot...?" I suggested.

She was silent at that.

"...Uh."

Shinobu was so quiet, it was making me feel nervous.

"So er... When's the hidden camera coming out? You aren't going to shout 'surprise' or something?"

"I'm not."

"Right."

I see. Well, this is obviously a prank. But without the little fanfare at the end and the reveal... I suppose it can't be.

The room was quiet for a few moments.

"This...really isn't a prank?" I asked.

"I already told you that, didn't I?"

More silence followed. It felt like the world was up and running twenty-four hours a day, seven days a week, three hundred and sixty-five days a year, always moving forwards, always spinning...but now a gear was loose somewhere, and a part of our world was down for maintenance.

As for what was running through my head—it was nothing at all. *There must be something seriously wrong with anyone who can actually get asked out by a high school girl and maintain proper brain function.*

Shinobu was the first to break the weird atmosphere that had settled around us. "So, what do you think? Will you go out with me?"

".................Come on," I said. "Reconsider." *I'm sure you can sense just how much wavering, hesitation, and inner conflict those six ellipses contained.*

"Why?"

"First of all, you're a high school student," I said.

"I am. What of it?"

"I mean... You know. It's a bit dodgy, isn't it? Right? It's gotta be against some law for grown adults to date minors. I don't want to be a criminal."

"It's okay, Mizuki-san. It's only against the law if you have sexual relations with a minor. There's no problem with pure, platonic relationships with marriage in mind."

"You barely go to school, but you've read up on *this* stuff, huh?"

"I look at the terms and conditions. I'm a YourTuber, after all."

I should've known. *Stepping right up to the line of what's legal and permissible is a YourTuber's bread and butter, isn't it?*

"The law might be okay with us dating, but I'm not," I told her.

"Why is that?"

"Well, what's gotten into you? Where's this coming from all of a sudden? What makes you want to date *me*?" I kept up a semblance of calm, but I was panicking on the inside—hence my asking the same question three times.

"I just started to like you, that's all," she told me. "So I wondered if you wanted to go out with me."

"When did I do anything that would make you like me?"

"I think you've got more going for you than the average boy or girl," she said.

This girl pushes her way into my house, gets all stalkery on me, and then I go save her life from those goblins... I get it. She's right, I have to admit there are quite a few points in my favor here. These developments are worthy of their own rom-com, and they're coming in fast!

"All right," I said. "I understand how you feel."

"You do? Then let's make it official."

"*No*, come on. Think it over. All these ups and downs, the storms you've had to endure these past few days, knocking you off balance... You've fallen for the suspension bridge effect—you only think you're in love because of all the stress. These feelings you've got? They're a misunderstanding. You've just got too much time on your hands right now. You were lying in bed, poking at your smartphone, and had this strange and terrible resolve well up inside you to date me, right?"

"Are you trying to tell me no or enter a speech contest with that answer?" she snapped back.

Look, I'm panicking right now! There are some people who talk way too much when they're confused and under pressure, and I'm absolutely one of them.

"But," she added, "isn't that just what love is?"

"What, we're trying to figure out the true meaning of love now?"

"If anyone's going to reconsider, it should be you, Mizuki-san," she pressed. "Listen, okay? You're a working adult, and a high school girl is asking you out. This kind of thing doesn't happen every day."

"I can hardly disagree with that."

"And I'm pretty cute too, aren't I?"

"You're a *minor* and I don't want to hurt your self-esteem," I conceded. "I'll agree with that."

"Also, I mean... Despite my looks, I've got kind of a big butt and big boobs, you know?"

"I don't know about that. Setting the objective truth aside, I'm going to withhold my agreement."

"I'm pretty accommodating when it comes to kinks too. I do read some of *those* kinds of comics," she argued.

"I'm starting to smell danger. Goodbye."

My lifetime record stood at one match, one defeat—but I stepped back with the swift motions of a martial artist and went to close the door. With a *thunk*, Shinobu jammed her white Abidas sneaker in the gap to stop me from locking her out. She slipped her fingers into the crack and strained to peek through the gap between the wall and the door like some terrifying yandere from hell.

"Let me ask again," she said. "Will you go out with me?"

"I'm sorry," I replied. "Please consider someone else."

"I think once we start dating, we should just like, come out and talk about all our fetishes and figure out what's okay and what's off the table," she began. "What do you think? It might avoid disappointment in the future, no? I've always wanted to do it like that, when I did someday get into a relationship with a man."

"Sorry, but please stop continuing this conversation like I agreed to start dating you. And especially don't talk about *that*. I didn't expect you to go there."

"Ah, I kind of like this side of you as well. I feel *totally* in love right now. Like, my heart's beating *so* fast."

"That's because this is a unique situation. Way *too* unique," I replied.

Our battle at the door continued for a few more moments until Shinobu made one last proposal.

"Then well, how about this? What if I were to...?"

3

THE NEXT DAY, MY FEELINGS STILL FRAYED, I RECEIVED a call. It was Carol, the captain of REA.

"Is this Mizuki Ryosuke?"

"It is. Nobody else uses this phone."

"Come over to my hotel."

"To your hotel? What for?" I asked.

"There's something I want to check. It's at..."

She went on to tell me the name and address of her hotel, and I got in my Celsiar to drive there. Carol was staying at the most expensive place in town, near the Omori Train Station. I found a parking space nearby and walked up to see Carol standing out in front. She was still wearing her full set of medieval fantasy armor, including the spiked helmet.

More than eccentric enough to attract some eyeballs... She looks like that English girl who looked like the "modern day Joan of Arc" that blew up on Tmitter with over a million retmeets after someone snapped a picture of her.

There were few people on the street, but none of them were quite managing to ignore her all the way. As I walked up to greet her, she stood completely motionless waiting for my arrival.

"You're late, Mizuki," she said bluntly. "When I call again, be here within ten minutes."

"Give me at least twenty, won't you?"

"If twenty minutes would allow you leeway, I take it that ten can be done. Now walk."

I did as I was told and followed her inside to an elevator. The bright red feather attached to her helmet caught my eye. Following her instructions from there, we arrived at her room. Not for a moment during this did Carol turn her back on me—preferring to tail me from behind and instruct me on where to go.

She seemed to be staying in the room alone. In terms of personal effects, there was a rolling suitcase in one corner, and a thin Bapple laptop on the desk, but aside from that, the room was bare.

"So what is it you wanted to check?" I asked. "Something about the dungeon? Did Horinomiya say something?"

"No. It's you I need to check." She then turned in my direction, reached out her hands, and started to touch me.

"Wh-what the heck?! Hey!" I protested.

"It's nothing to be concerned about. Calm down," she insisted.

Her expression unchanging, she moved her hands to my waist, then up to my arms. She was wearing fingerless gloves of some kind. Once she gave my clothes a once over, she tried to reach under my shirt.

"H-hey!" I protested. "Wait just a minute!"

"I need to do this. Stay still."

She ran her fingertips over my bare skin, poking at the muscles under my shirt like she was taking mental measurements. The weird ticklish feeling made me shake.

The blonde-haired, blue-eyed, iron-faced beauty was running her fingers all over my body. Even so, there was nothing sexual about it at all, I had to admit. It was more like a doctor's visit than anything else.

"Hmph. Your stats are unchanged," she said. "It doesn't seem like you've raised your strength."

"S-so what?"

"When there's a gap between your base values and stat values, that can cause problems in an emergency."

Carol's hands stretched down to my legs. She carefully stroked my inner thigh, then the outside, and dug her fingers into the muscles, applying pressure from above. She crouched down and started touching my calves too.

"Your agility probably hasn't changed either, eh? Have you leveled up?" she asked.

"Just once. Level 18 to 19."

"What did you spend your points in?"

"All three into Stamina," I explained.

"You have martial arts experience?"

"Nothing to write home about."

Not taking her eyes off me, she pointed at the neatly made bed beside her. "Sit. Turn and face me."

"Hey... What's the point in checking all this anyway? Why can't you just ask?"

"I don't want to have to deal with being lied to. I at least want an accurate assessment of your natural strength and agility."

"I'm not gonna lie to you," I replied.

"Some have lied to me in the past," she began. "In the depths of a dungeon, the difference between expected stats and reality can determine whether one lives or dies. Now sit."

I reluctantly sat down at the edge of the bed. She slipped her knee into the gap between my legs, and put both hands around my head, holding it in place. She then brought her face in so close I thought she was about to kiss me, but Carol only stared at me intently instead.

"S-so what's next...?" I asked meekly.

"Stay still. Look directly into my eyes. Don't look away."

She was so close I could feel her breath. I looked into her big pupils as instructed. She had sharp double eyelids, and beautiful, blue-colored irises. Her sapphire eyes then turned black and shrunk down to a vertical slit, like the eyes of a snake.

"Scale Eyes."

Her snake eyes looked like unpleasant color contacts and having them so close made me break out in a cold sweat. It scared me...or rather, made me feel like she could see right through me. The whole process lasted ten seconds, more or less. When it was over, she released my head, and her eyes went back to their usual brilliant blue.

"That's enough. I have what I need," she said. "You can leave now."

"Hey, wait a second! I don't have to put up with this." I got up from the bed and closed in on her—she was shorter than I was, so it wasn't hard. "What *was* that? I don't have any idea what you just did to me, and you think this was fair?"

"I didn't *do* anything to you," she countered. "I was checking you over to obtain the information I needed."

"Then I want some information in return. What was that thing you just did with your eyes? It sounds like you already *knew* what my stats were before you checked, anyway. What's going on?"

"...Mizuki." She glared at me, and for a moment I felt like a frog under the eyes of a predator. My whole body stiffened up and I shrank away.

Ugh! And she's so much smaller than me too! She's just some little blonde-haired girl playing dress up as a knight from the Middle Ages!

Even so, the aura she was giving off was terribly strong. *Is this just the difference in our levels, or is there some skill she's using to intimidate me? Is she just going to force me out of her room now? Damn it. I let her get away with this, and now she's even more sure of her superiority than ever... She calls me here with no explanation, feels me up like some toy, then tries to throw me out when she's done with me?*

If I stay quiet here, I'm not just letting her take all the initiative... I'm giving her the power to end my life. Next time this little brat opens her mouth, I'm going off on her! I'm gonna say it! I don't care if she is the strongest adventurer in Britain, she has to take me more seriously!!! I was always quiet at my old company! I always just shut my mouth and listened to what my superiors told me!

Carol opened her mouth to speak at last. "You're right," she said calmly.

"Shut up!!!" I yelled.

"Huh?"

"Huh?" I said, surprised myself.

Both of us froze for a moment. After a few awkward seconds, she continued—looking a little shaken by my outburst.

"I meant that to build a good relationship of trust between us... I do agree that we should exchange information... Do you have an objection to that?" she asked.

"Eh? No... Uh, you're right. Yeah. Right. I thought so."

"But did you...just tell me to shut up?" she asked.

"N-no? I didn't say anything like that..." I lied. "Maybe your Auto-Translate malfunctioned?"

"Then why did you suddenly call out like that?"

"Well, er I... I said, 'Yeah, all right!'"

She seemed skeptical. "Really?"

"Are you sure your Auto-Translate skill's working right?"

4

"EXCHANGING INFORMATION" MEANT THAT CAROL allowed me to see her stat screen.

LEVEL **48**	
HP **19**	MP **5**
STRENGTH **36**	STAMINA **20**
WISDOM **19**	INTELLIGENCE **76**
RESILIENCE **15**	AGILITY **65**
CHARM **18**	

"How come your Intelligence and Agility are so high?" I asked.

"Those are my primary attributes," she explained. "Agility boosts the speed of my reflexes when using skills and gives me superhuman abilities in combat. With my other skills activated, I can dodge bullets fired at me and even parry them with my sword."

"Amazing..."

"All of my other attributes are minimal as a result, so you could call me a one-trick pony. The other members make up for the things I lack."

"What do you use Intelligence for?" I asked. "You've got that up to 76."

"Intelligence is connected to Analysis Skills. I fight by analyzing my enemies' weak points, then striking decisively before they can make a move."

"Analysis?"

"My main skill, Scale Eyes, is an Analysis Skill."

Scale Eyes
Rank S - Level ?? Required (Unique Skill)
Analysis Skill
Concentrate on targets within line of sight to perform
    analysis.
Provides information on analyzed targets.

So Carol's Scale Eyes skill is based on her intelligence stat? She's at 76 so that's insanely high. It lets her analyze a target's base stats, weaknesses, and armor values. That lets her come up with the perfect plan to handle them before starting a fight.

"I also use a variety of close combat physical damage and Sword Skills in battle. I have an 'Albert helmet' from down in the dungeons as my headpiece. I also receive a set bonus, known as Full Dress, from having the complete set of gear, but I'd prefer to avoid going into too much detail on that."

"Thanks," I said. "I think I understand things a bit better now."

So she isn't just wearing that because she's into cosplay... That's a real-life set of armor for going into battle. I do wonder why she needs to wear it in this hotel, though. But hey, maybe it's just a fashion choice, like how junior high and high schoolers suddenly start wanting to wear sunglasses for no reason... I won't pry any further.

"When we were moving through the hotel, I performed an analysis on your back, and then again when you turned to face me. I know all of your stats and have information on each of your skills," she told me.

"I would've appreciated a heads up, but fine. I forgive you."

"Had you shown signs of resisting, I would have just taken note of your stats and kept the information to myself. But since you cooperated, I now have all the intel I need and can prioritize the smooth execution of our current mission. That is why I shared my stats with you, nothing more. I trust you'll keep them strictly confidential."

That said, from the way Carol was lounging in a chair in the corner of the hotel room now, she seemed supremely confident that it wouldn't matter much either way.

"Leak that morsel of information if you want but you'll never shake us from the top spot" is more the vibe I'm getting.

"Understood," I answered her.

"I'm sorry for touching you like that. I apologize if it made you uncomfortable."

"No, you don't need to apologize for that." *Most guys would probably consider it a reward. Hey, now I've calmed down a bit, why don't you do it again?*

I'm kidding.

"What's this Skillbook in your possession? Can I ask what the skill does?"

"Sure. There's a lot I don't know about it yet myself..."

I activated Skillbook, and explained to Carol what I knew about it. Since she knew way more about dungeons than I did, I figured she might know something about the ability or at least be able to give me some advice on using it.

"I see... It allows you to ignore the required level of skills, then," she deduced.

"Seems like it, but I still don't really get how it works. I don't have many skills yet, and I don't want to waste charges testing it out."

"It's an interesting skill, and its effects could change considerably depending on how you use it." She made a sudden, mid-sentence switch into fluent English. *"It would probably be more accurate to say..."*

That must be one of the Auto-Translate malfunctions she mentioned.

Carol showed no sign that she noticed the blip and continued on. "Skillbook... There are *absolutely* diabolical ways in which you could make use of it, I'm sure. I'm very interested in it."

"Really?" I was happy to hear that.

I might have been intimidated into agreeing to Horinomiya's request, but getting to go down into a dungeon with an elite party like REA was a dream opportunity. It would allow me to try out Skillbook in some real situations, and if I could understand more about how it actually works...that would help me plan for the future. And if this skill turned out to be too much for me to handle, I might be able to ask Carol to help me determine an asking price to actually sell the thing.

After we went through several more topics of discussion and arrangements, Carol sighed.

"But at present, I don't think you're going to be much use in a fight," she said.

Well, compared to the strongest adventuring party in Britain, that made sense. *I don't have any dungeon gear, and all I can do is make fire shoot of this book six more times—I can hardly complain if they want me on the bench.*

"You did walk around the Omori Dungeon's upper levels for some time though, didn't you?" she asked.

"Well, yeah. I had my reasons."

"Then we'll find some use for you as a navigator. Leave the fighting to us, and you can focus on guiding us through the dungeon."

"Gotcha. That works for me."

Carol stood up from her chair, her armor clinking as she moved. "Right then, Mizuki. I know this is a simple mission for you, a stroll around a dungeon following us as we go. Just try not to get in our way."

Ugh. She had manners, but her words sure did have some bite to them. *I guess she's just being honest with me—a reflection of the absolute confidence she seems to have in herself. It's not like she's actively trying to look down on or belittle me... She just says exactly what she's thinking, straight-up and unedited. That's just who she is, huh.*

"Well, all right then. Since you're the strongest party of adventurers in Britain, I'll do my best to learn everything I can from you."

"Don't let REA down."

We shook on it. Under the metal gauntlet, her hand was soft and delicate—the hand of a young girl.

When I left Carol's hotel room, I found the burly guys from before leaning against the walls of the hallway outside. I had never been greeted by a more intense group of people in my life.

"Little baby adventurer just went in to play with the boss, huh?"

"Hmph. Just don't drag us down in there, yeah?"

One spoke in English. *"What a sissy. Bring it on."*

"Go home and eat your mum's toad in the hole, kid."

"Hey, you're super cute. If you aren't busy, would you like to come to my room tonight for some drinks?"

The hallway was stifling hot, and I was assaulted by voices from both sides. I ignored them all and kept walking. Carol had mentioned that some of them didn't have the Auto-Translate skill—I heard a few lines of English mixed in, but at native speed, I couldn't really tell what they were saying.

Nothing good, though, I'm fairly sure of that. Also, this American... well, foreign way of taunting doesn't really land with Japanese people, even when it's translated. Cultural differences, I suppose?

I took the elevator down to the ground floor, left the hotel, and went back to my car. I clicked the engine on and checked my smartphone before setting off.

Whoa, that's a lot of Lain messages. I couldn't stand having unanswered notifications on my phone, so I was always checking it. *The day I glance over at someone else's and see several hundred notifications is the day I finally lose the plot...*

But that day, my finger froze as I went to answer the twenty pings I had.

The last one was from Shinobu—*"What are you doing?"*—and there were missed calls too. I hesitated, but my policy of never putting anything off kicked in, and I called her.

The phone didn't fully ring once before she picked up.

"Ah, hello. This is Shinobu."

"Yeah, what's up?"

"What do you mean what's up? You're the one who called me, Mizuki-san."

"You're the one who left me the damn missed calls."

I heard her snickering from the other end of the line. *"Well. I just wondered what you were doing, is all."*

"Right now... All kinds of things. Some things I can't talk about."

"Of course, right. You are *an adventurer, after all."*

I paused for a moment. "Look, Shinobu," I said. "I appreciate that you like me, I do... But, y'know. You're still in high school. There's that suspension bridge effect I talked about, remember? The bit of your brain that controls love is going into overdrive right now, that's all this is. You're taking a break from YourTube and you've got nothing else to do, right? This is just a phase."

"I am *serious about this,*" she insisted.

"I'm happy to hear that. Just go to school, okay? Then we'll talk."

"All right. I'll go when my suspension's over."

"You do that."

"If I go to school, then *will you go out with me?"*

"That's not what I'm saying, no. I'm just telling you to go."

"This isn't fair."

"Is that the problem?"

I heard her laughing again. *"Hey, Mizuki-san?"*

"What?"

"I know I can be needy. Don't let that bother you too much, okay?"

"I'm kinda scared of how fast you'll turn to stalking again, so you're gonna have to keep that in check for me," I said.

"I'll get better. Oh, and don't forget your promise."

"I didn't agree to anything."

"When I get my adventuring license, go out with me, okay? It's a promise."

"I'm not clear on what those two things have to do with each other."

Shinobu hung up after that. I stepped on the gas and the car started to move—I switched the radio to the news, details of events happening all across Japan.

"...A bank in Omori City, Hokkaido, was robbed late last night, with the culprits making off with several million yen in cash... The police are pursuing leads that a special skill may have been used to commit the crime..."

5

SEVERAL MORE MEETINGS WITH REA HAPPENED, and at last, it was the day before we were scheduled to head into the Omori Dungeon together. That day, I found myself standing with Carol inside the Omori City Police Station. This was where firearms and other weapons were temporarily stored and managed. Before going into the dungeon, we first came here to retrieve weapons. Then, we would ride to the dungeon under strict police escort and supervision in their patrol cars.

There was typically a reservation and scheduling system in place for dungeon entry, but with no such system up and running in Omori City just yet, it seemed to be Horinomiya's influence behind the scenes that was getting us in.

Inside the weapons facility, and under the watchful eye of several officers, Carol explained to me the weapons we would be taking with us.

"This is an M1911. You Japanese call it a Colt Government," she said, handing me the pistol.

Its barrel was pulled back, and the gun wasn't loaded. The live ammunition and magazines were stored and managed separately from the actual guns. "You're going to be carrying this when we're down in the dungeon. I would rather give you a lecture with a real firearm and ammo, but this'll have to do. You know the basics of how it works, don't you?" she asked.

"More or less."

"Don't worry, you won't have any chance to actually use it. If you're firing that thing, it means everybody else is already dead."

Perhaps it was because it was missing the magazine, but the gun felt much lighter in my hands than I expected it to.

"I'm not a military nerd, but I do know this is a pretty old pistol," I said.

"That makes it reliable," she commented.

"I figured we'd be using something more up to date. A Glock or something, maybe."

"Small caliber weapons can't even put down goblins. This government uses bigger .45 ACP bullets—to be honest, this isn't a Colt Government at all."

"It's not? Then why did you call it that?" I asked.

"I thought that would be easier for you to understand. This particular gun was developed based on the M1911, but it's a custom model built for dungeon exploration. It handles a little differently than the M1911, so don't go looking up guides on the internet—just remember what I'm telling you."

"Oh. All right then." *If I had my way, I'd really prefer to have an assault rifle or a shotgun in my hands though.*

I must've had that dissatisfied look on my face, as Carol smiled at me reassuringly, like she just read my mind.

"Don't worry, you're the only one who'll be carrying a pistol. REA's assault team are armed with shotguns and assault rifles."

"Are you using a gun as well?"

"I'll be armed with one for emergencies, but guns don't suit my skills very well," she explained. "My main weapon is something different."

She proceeded to give me a lecture on how to use the pistol. Even without bullets, holding and pointing a real gun made the little kid in me come out. After her lecture was done, Carol went to fetch more equipment.

"Here's your stab-proof Keplar fiber vest. And here're your helmet and night-vision goggles. You'll be wearing all this tomorrow. Last up, combat boots. Horinomiya had several pairs made to fit your feet, so see which ones you can walk in."

I tried out each of the five pairs of boots she laid out for me and chose the ones that fit the best. The stab-proof vest was lighter and easier to move around in than I expected, but the material's thinness only ended up making me worry about its effectiveness.

"I like that it's comfortable, but am I going to be okay in a vest this thin...?"

"Of course you aren't going to be *okay*."

"What?" I asked.

"A stronger vest made with metal would just slow you down," she explained. "If you're put in a position where you have to face down a monster, you'd be far better off running than fighting. If you can't run, you'll die. What you've got there is a security blanket, nothing more."

We left the police station, and Carol turned to look over at me.

"Right then, Mizuki," she said. "Tomorrow's going to go just as we discussed in our meetings. Give the documents I emailed you another look as well."

"Do you have a bit more time?" I asked.

"What is it?"

I walked over to her, suppressing the emotion in my voice as I spoke. "There's some more information I want to share with you."

"What is it? You already told me about the encounter with the dragon."

"It's about Horinomiya, actually," I said. "Something that's been on my mind. And I'd like this to stay between us, if possible."

"Between the two of us, you mean?" Carol then tilted her head at me, took a glance at the van waiting behind her, and turned back to me.

"I know a lot of your teammates don't think much of me," I said. "I don't want this to get too complicated."

"Tell me what you have to say."

"It's a little complicated so I need to explain it properly. I might be worrying too much, and so I really just want your thoughts on the matter."

Carol thought for a moment and gave a signal to the waiting van. "All right, I'll hear you out," she said. "I'm hungry, though. Let's go somewhere for some food."

With Carol in the passenger seat of my car, I drove toward the train station.

"What do you want to eat?" I asked her.

"I hear that Japanese ramen's good."

"Let's go with that then."

I stopped the car at a residential building just in front of the station that had been converted into a ramen place. The other customers and staff inside were shocked by Carol's high-quality cosplay. After we bought our meal tickets from the machine and sat down at a table, I took out my tablet and showed her the screen.

"What's this?" she asked.

"Horinomiya's large shareholder report."

"Large shareholding *what*?"

I began to explain. "Horinomiya is the company president of Horimiya Group, but he's also the largest shareholder. Major shareholders have to disclose the selling and buying of shares to the FSA. This is to protect smaller investors, and to..."

"W-wait a minute." Carol held up her hand to tell me to stop, and I cut my rapid-fire explanation short. "I don't understand what you're talking about..."

"Huh? Um, well, this document is..."

"You used to work for an investment bank, right, Mizuki?"

"Yeah, I did."

"So maybe *you're* good with these things... I know a lot about clearing dungeons, but aside from that...I'm sixteen years old." Carol looked a little troubled, her slender shoulders fidgeting back and forth. "Could you maybe...break down the difficult parts for me?"

"...Ah."

She's right. I'm always talking about this stuff with my back straight, dealing with the particulars of this business... But despite being the captain of the strongest party of adventurers in all of the UK, Carol's just a teenager. She always seems so confident and determined, so I was talking to her like a business partner my own age, or even a boss at work.

"Well, getting to the point," I said. "Looking at this document, we can see roughly where Horinomiya's putting his money."

"Okay. And?"

"It's kind of in my job description, I couldn't help but take a look... Some of these movements are a little suspicious."

Horinomiya had been borrowing money from major banks for three years, using his own stocks as collateral. The amount he was borrowing had increased year after year, and when combined with stock sales, he seemed to be accumulating a huge amount of funds for something.

"Aren't the presidents of all big corporations just like that?" she asked.

"I suppose that's one way of looking at it. The way he uses his money, and the amounts he deals in, are too different from our situations to make a good comparison. But analyzing these moves carefully, to me, it looks like his financial position is just getting worse and worse."

From this large shareholding report, I could see evidence that his stock positions were in jeopardy, and he was using his collateral to compensate. He made a series of moves that you never would under normal circumstances, and I could clearly see the month when his behind-the-scenes deals allowed him to pull through. It also might have had something to do with their failure to align themselves with a certain foreign industry, which led Horimiya Group to its greatest one-day drop in stock price in the company's history... *But I'm not explaining that to Carol, it'd only make this more complicated.*

"So you're saying that...Horinomiya doesn't have any money?" she asked.

"Well it's a bit different from you or me being broke... But it's possible he's in a dangerous position right now. If there's some accident that means his collateral has to be liquidated, he could go bankrupt in a day. He might be on the edge right now," I explained.

"Why does he need so much more money? He should have plenty."

"He started accumulating funds three years ago," I explained. "About the same time he began exploring dungeons too, apparently. It could be he's spending cash like water, hiring adventurers like us to explore dungeons all over the world. More than he can handle, even."

"But why?" she asked. "If he wants to stop worrying about the future, why not slow down his spending?"

"Might be that he really does have a serious illness... Something he can't tell anybody else about."

Carol went silent, thinking about something. The ramen we ordered arrived, and she picked out a pair of chopsticks. She gazed down at the two pieces of black dried seaweed topping and the thick ramen soup with oil floating on its surface.

"How am I supposed to eat this?" she asked.

"However you like."

"What are those?" she then asked, pointing to the condiments.

"White pepper, black pepper, garlic, and ginger."

I shook some pepper over mine and mixed in some raw garlic— Carol did the same. We ate together. Carol wasn't even good enough at using chopsticks for me to feign a compliment.

"It's good," she said. "The soup's really rich."

"Glad you like it."

"About Horinomiya... I'll ask my manager about the situation."

"Thanks. Can't have us risking our lives down in some dungeon only for him to ghost us when we get back up to the surface," I said.

"But when you say Horinomiya is in a dangerous position... You don't mean he could go under today or tomorrow, do you?" asked Carol.

"I don't think so, no. This is all just speculation anyway."

"I don't expect it'll be a problem then. I've been denied payment after completing missions before. I'll ensure you get yours as well, if it comes to that. Don't concern yourself with this. Focus on tomorrow's dungeon clearing."

After Carol and I finished our big-picture discussion, I returned to my cheap apartment and found Shinobu crouching outside the door. I couldn't suppress a noise of annoyance when I saw her.

It's not that I hated Shinobu or anything...but finding a high school girl waiting for you when you least expected it was tough. Anyone would struggle to come up with an appropriate reaction.

But when Shinobu saw me, she jumped up with such agility that I felt like I just snuck up on a cat.

"Oh! Mizuki-san! Hey, welcome home!" she greeted me.

"No. Come on now. This isn't normal, right?"

"What isn't normal?"

"What are you doing outside my apartment?" I asked.

"I just went to the convenience store, and when I swung by, you weren't home," she said, showing me a plastic bag as evidence.

"So?"

"So I waited for you."

"How long?" I pressed.

"About...an hour, maybe?"

"What are you, a stalker?"

"Mizuki-san, you have such a casual way of hurting people."

"Sorry. I shouldn't have said it like that," I apologized. *I guess that was a bit blunt.* "So, what do you want?"

"I just came here to see you, that's all."

"Right... Well, good job."

"Is 'good job' really the right thing to say there?" she asked me.

I didn't really think so either, but I didn't know how to address a high schooler who just waited for an hour outside my apartment for no reason in particular.

She continued speaking. "So, anyway. Aren't you interested to know what I bought at the convenience store?"

"Not really."

"You *should* be interested."

"Fine, I'll ask. What did you get?" *Pudding, right? It's probably pudding.*

"Rubbers. The thin ones."

I shouldn't have asked. "Go home, Shinobu. Go. Home."

She ignored that. "You know, I've been thinking. Wouldn't this be over faster if we just did it? Just once, for the time being, I mean. I just *know* I can captivate you, Mizuki-san, I'm super confident."

"Yeah, maybe you could, but go home. Go." I repeated myself and grabbed Shinobu by the shoulders.

"Mizuki-saaaan?" she wailed. "Won't you think about this some more? I really do like you, Mizuki-san, like seriously I do. When I'm at home you're all I can think about. It gets me *super* turned on."

"Hey, I didn't need to know that last bit."

"You know, I seriously don't plan on ever letting you get away, Mizuki-san. You get that, right? I don't know if I'll ever find anyone as good as you as long as I live, yeah? Won't you go on a date with me, just once? Like, as a trial."

"I don't need a trial period."

"Well, you can't just return me after you've used me once, you know?"

"Then that's not even a trial period."

"Huh? Don't tell me, Mizuki-san... You wanted to sleep with me just to see what it would feel like? To throw me away once you're done with me, like I could just be returned to the shop whenever the mood struck you?"

"You're the one who mentioned a trial."

"Aaahhhh... I waited over an hour, you know! You aren't even going to offer me a cup of coffee, are you? I think, like, you could *at least* let me inside for a while."

"You deciding to wait out here isn't my fault," I said.

"Oh, a drive somewhere sure would be nice. I'd *love* if you would take me somewhere. Your car's so cool, and it's just sitting there, Mizuki-san..."

"Huh? You really think my car's cool?"

I was happy to hear her compliment my beloved Celsiar. *It's the same with all guys, I guess. We're a hundred times happier when someone randomly says they like our cars or collections of stuff than when we actually get random compliments about ourselves.*

"I do, yes."

"Thanks." *I'm always running that thing through the car wash, even when it's only a little dirty.*

"So you'll take me on a drive?" she asked.

"Well, if it isn't too far..."

"All right."

"But where do you even want to go?"

"A hotel or something?"

"Nope, it's time for you to go home."

"No!" Shinobu wailed as I pushed her away. "I messed up there at the end! Forget I said anything..."

Meeting with one of Japan's leading businessmen and the strongest party of adventurers in Britain... That's how my everyday life went that day, planning for the huge mission to come.

The next day, however...we were finally going to enter the Omori Dungeon.

I never expected what would happen next. At that point in time, none of us did—not me, not Carol, not Horinomiya... Nobody knew what was coming.

CHAPTER 8

AN INNATE NAVIGATION SKILL I WASN'T BORN WITH

1

PROGRESS WAS WELL UNDERWAY ON CONSTRUCTION of a proper facility to manage the Omori Dungeon. There was just a steel frame up for the outer walls, but it already gave me a clear idea of what the finished building would look like. Horinomiya's REA and I were getting ready to enter the dungeon inside the unfinished building, surrounded by police cars, JSDF vehicles from a nearby garrison, and countless other staff.

Carol's burly teammates were kitted out with rough vests and armed with the kinds of weapons I only ever saw in the movies. Once basic preparations were done, they still weren't even allowed to touch their empty firearms. They were only permitted to load them once we were inside the dungeon itself. The number of live rounds that could be brought inside was strictly regulated down to the last bullet.

"Mizuki Ryosuke. One pistol. Twenty-one live rounds in total. Three magazines." The JSDF employee checked my adventuring license and handed me my pistol. I placed it into my holster—it was still unloaded.

When accepting firearms from the officials, we weren't allowed any sudden or unnecessary movements. Once the staff had confirmed my pistol was in its holster, I was handed three empty magazines. I counted out the twenty-one bullets in front of a staff member, then loaded them into the magazines. It was my first time holding live rounds, and I had a hard time getting the bullets inside.

One of the JSDF guys who seemed higher ranked than the others noticed me struggling and came over to help.

"You ever touch a gun before?" he asked, helping me with the magazines. He looked to be in his mid-thirties; the patch on his collar had a single star with two thick horizontal lines underneath it.

He seems pretty high up... Not that I know anything about JSDF ranks.

"I'm just here as a guide," I told him. "I don't actually plan on firing this thing."

He smiled. "If you don't have to fire it, then it's best you don't."

He even showed me how to tuck the magazines away into my vest. There were all kinds of pockets for them, but he placed them all on my left side, close to my waist.

"You're right-handed, aren't you?" he asked.

"Yes."

"Then this is the way."

He then patted me on the back and walked off, satisfied that I was ready.

"Hey, um," I called after him. "Thanks a lot."

"It's okay. Take care down there."

"Could I ask your name?"

He pulled the brim of his dark green military cap down over his eyes and grinned at me. "11th Brigade, Major Himata."

With that, he left, and with so little to get ready compared to everybody else, I stood there with nothing more to do. I took the opportunity to try muttering something to Kessie with my mind—the fairy was hidden in one of my pockets.

<Um...Kessie? Can you hear me?>

<Loud and clear! I hear you, Zukky-san!> she replied.

<Okay, cool. It works.>

Nobody else was aware of the fairy in my pocket.

To be honest, I might've been down in the dungeon once before...but actually navigating this thing was going to be all on Kessie. I mean, I walked around this place while it was still shifting and changing, so I knew almost nothing about the actual layout.

I had Kessie keep her ears open for my thoughts, always reading my mind telepathically so that we could talk whenever we needed to. I practiced chatting with her without using my mouth while I waited for the others to get ready.

<All right. I'm counting on you, Kessie.>

<Roger that! Leave it to me!>

<I'll buy you a DVD box set of How About Thursday? *if you can pull this off.>*

<Awesome! Let's watch it together!> she cheered.

There were five members of REA entering the dungeon that day—and with me, that made six. The REA members, apart from Carol herself, had rifles and shotguns, along with several magazines of ammo stuck into each of their vests. Only one of them seemed to be dressed significantly differently from the others—our combat medic, there to help us out if anyone got injured.

And in the center of them all stood the young blonde-haired girl, Carol.

She was dressed as she always was, like a knight from the Middle Ages, complete with that red feather sticking out from the top of her spiked helmet. She wasn't holding a rifle, shotgun, or even a handgun... Instead, she had an ancient-looking, two-handed, double-edged sword, with a metal sword guard jutting out on either side of it.

I had already heard in our meetings that Carol, as a sixteen-year-old, didn't have an adventuring license in Japan or in her home country. On paper, she was entering as an associate of one of the licensed men in her party.

When it came about time for us to enter the dungeon, Horinomiya walked over to speak with us all. "Well then, I'm counting on you."

"Please, don't worry about us," replied Carol, shooting a sharp glance in his direction. "Though even if we manage to clear this Omori Dungeon in its entirety, there is no guarantee it will yield the item you're looking for."

Horinomiya's usual smile faltered a little at that, and there was a small flush of panic. "I am aware... But I *do* believe you will find it. I just know you will."

"Believe whatever you like, but all we're giving you are the items we find down there," Carol said simply. "That's what's in the contract."

Working adventurer parties like REA contracted with investors and big businesses, entering dungeons with their support and financial backing.

Considering how valuable some of the rare dungeon resources you can find are, I supposed some people would think this operation could be self-financing without the whole patronage system. In reality, though, there was no guarantee that a party would find any useful resources down in the dungeons, and a group operating on the scale of REA required quite a lot of financing to keep up and running. They might not necessarily break even on any given dungeon clearing, and connections to powerful brokers and big businesses were needed to smoothly navigate the complex array of dungeon rules and regulations to actually get down there.

For those reasons, REA chose to be compensated by the businesses and investors they contracted with rather than self-finance their operations. In return for giving up almost all of the resources they found to their clients, they were promised a set reward regardless of the loot they brought in—not to mention a huge bonus if they found the specific item that Horinomiya had requested.

"Well then, I'm counting on you all. You as well, Mizuki-san," said the businessman.

"Ahem... Well, like Carol said... I can't promise you anything," I remarked.

"I'm sure you'll find it. You *have* to." There was a note of panic in his voice. "This may be our last chance."

"Hm? What do you mean by th—"

But my words were cut off by the blaring of a siren, and everyone not a member of our party was cordoned off from the area near the dungeon's entrance. We were surrounded by armed JSDF soldiers on all sides, who looked at us and our assortment of firearms with caution.

A nearby police officer began to make the official announcement.

"10:30 a.m. Licensed adventurers include four members of REA, and Mizuki Ryosuke. One associate, Carol Middleton. You may now enter the Omori Dungeon!"

2

I BET ANY AVERAGE JAPANESE GUY LIKE ME WHO knows a fair bit about games, manga, and anime already has a fair idea of what a party of adventurers setting off to clear a dungeon would look like. I mean, there's the swordsman who cuts down enemies on the front lines, the mage who supports him, the archer at the back dealing all the damage, and the priest who heals the party's injuries—just like in the JRPGs.

But now, here in modern-day Japan, watching a real working party of adventurers handle a dungeon clearing was nothing like in the fantasy stories.

"Gob! Go-gob!"

The goblin lurking in a shadow at the end of the hallway was met with a burst of fire from our party's assault rifles. It was killed immediately.

The two members of REA's assault team were always in front. One had a shotgun, and the other was armed with an assault rifle. They kept their guns drawn as we moved through the dungeon, shooting down monsters that approached us, neither threatening nor warning them at all before they took their perfect shots. Carol, armed with her sword, and our combat medic armed with his rifle, walked behind them—both ready to step in at a moment's notice if there should be some sudden problem.

Bringing up the rear of our group was a man even larger than the others, facing the other direction to watch our backs. He seemed to trust the assault team immensely as he never turned to look back at them, not dropping his guard for a moment even when gunfire started. He had spare firearms on his back in case the one in his hands should break down, and he had plenty of spare ammunition too.

I was positioned a little ahead of our burly rear guard and was positioned as far off to one flank as possible so I wouldn't interfere with their formation.

"What do you think of REA's dungeon clearing?" Carol asked me.

"You all seem more like special forces than adventurers."

"It might appear that way. This is just one way to search."

"What do you mean?" I asked.

"Just keep watching. Oh, and this is the way down to the deeper levels, right?"

"Ah..."

I took a moment to call Kessie telepathically.

<Kessie! You awake?>

<Of course I'm awake!> she replied.

<Which path do we take? You know the way?>

<You want to go down to the deeper levels, don't you? They're over that way!>

<...You're gonna have to be more specific than "that way," Kessie!>

As Kessie and I continued our conversation inside my head, Carol turned to look back at me.

"What is it, Mizuki? Which way do we go?"

"Ah, ahem! I know! I do know the way, really!"

"Then tell me, quickly," she snapped. "That's the reason you're here."

"Ahh... Let me see..."

I returned to my telepathic conversation, concentrating hard on not actually saying the words aloud. It was hard to get used to it—there was a real trick to putting your thoughts into full sentences.

<Kessie! Tell me in a way I can understand!> I pleaded.

<I already sent it to you! You didn't get it?!>

<Huh? What do you mean?>

Then, I felt it—a vague feeling floating into my mind about the right way to go. I had no idea where I was and was even unsure of what kind of rock was beneath my feet...but at the same time, I had a strange feeling that I knew the way to go. It was a soft, unreliable, vague, and hazy sort of sense of my position in the cave.

"Ah! It's that way!" I exclaimed. "Yep! Turn right at that intersection there!"

"All right... What's gotten into you, Mizuki? Nerves?" Carol asked.

"Y-yeah... Must be nerves. I'm still getting the hang of all this." *The hang of being telepathically ordered around by the fairy hiding in my pocket, that is.*

But when I thought about it, I realized I really was relying on Kessie for almost everything down here, ever since I first set foot in this dungeon. *It's not like I'm trying to rely on her or anything...but when push comes to shove, I really need her, and I've come to take it for granted that she'll sort things out for me. I've gotta make sure to thank her once this mission's over.*

<You know I can hear everything you're thinking, don't you?!>

Ugh, don't just slide into my thoughts like we're having a conversation! Damn, that's scary. This sure is a new sensation.

I kept Kessie in my pocket with her telepathy switch turned on. She guided me and I guided REA as their navigator, and in short order we arrived at the entrance to the depths of the dungeon.

Really, this felt like no time at all. It was kind of like...oh? The upper levels are cleared? The first stage of this dungeon's already over?

It must really have been out of the ordinary for us to have made it this fast because Carol and the other four members of REA couldn't hide their surprise at our progress either.

"I never thought we would arrive so quickly..." she mumbled, narrowing her eyes skeptically.

"Did we not make a single wrong turn up there?" asked one of her teammates.

"We didn't even meet any boss creatures in the upper levels," noted Carol. "This must have been the shortest and best route available."

"That navigation was incredible. He even accounted for the dungeon's automatic shifts."

After a brief conversation with her party members, Carol walked towards me, determination in every step.

"Mizuki. I've made a decision."

"Huh? About what?"

"Once this mission is over, come join us in REA. We'll hire you as a regular to navigate for us. Whatever you're asking, we'll pay it."

"M-me?" I stuttered.

"Of course you. You only wandered around this dungeon once, but you managed to accurately map out its structure... And you've even accounted for the way its shape has shifted over time when guiding us around."

No way, I didn't do any of that! I just followed the instructions of the fairy in my pocket.

Carol continued praising me. "It's rare, truly rare, that people like you appear. You have a skill that doesn't appear on your stat screen—an innate talent for navigation. It's as if you've got a radar-like, intense understanding of this space. An ability to predict and understand its structure and pathways at a single glance... Then, you can choose the ideal path, planning the route in your head. You might have run into trouble the first time you delved down here, but nevertheless... The reason you made it back up to the surface is that innate ability to guide which you have within you."

That's not right at all. You're analyzing my abilities there, but you've got it all wrong. There's a fairy who's really into that Downtown *show on TV—she's the one who showed me the way out!*

<Who cares about that?> Kessie chimed in. *<Let's leave this misunderstanding be!>*

Please stop jumping into my thoughts like that. It's way more shocking than I think you understand to suddenly have another person in your head!

"I think I finally understand why Horinomiya hired you now," mused Carol. "Hmph. You're a rare find, a real discovery... All the money in the world could never buy the unique talent you have. I never expected to find someone like you in an island nation so far east..."

Nobody had ever showered me with so many compliments, and while the experience was novel, I couldn't find any joy in her words at all.

Then the soldier-looking types from REA came over and began to speak to me like they saw me in a completely new light.

"Heh... I was hard on you in the meetings, but I always trusted ya, kid."

What? Don't try and gaslight me now. I remember what you said about my mom's "toad in the hole."

"You've developed so fast. I sure was right to believe in you."

Do you mind giving me some concrete examples of when you ever believed in me? You totally ignored me in all those meetings we had together.

I couldn't understand the one speaking English to me. "You're super cute. Do you like art museums? I know a great exhibition in Sapporo. What are your plans on Saturday?"

You've gotta buy yourself an Auto-Translate skill, seriously!

Things seemed to be getting out of hand, so I looked to Carol for salvation.

"Well, anyway!" I said. "Let's talk about all that later. Should we get on with the mission?"

"Ah, of course. What was I thinking? It's unlike me to have gotten so excited." After saying that, Carol grabbed my arm and stood with me at the front of the group.

"...Carol? Why are you holding my arm?"

"Well, because you're mine now. Now then, which way do we go?"

"What? No, I'm not."

I was still stunned when the burly REA rear guard nudged my shoulder.

"The boss has taken a real liking to you, eh? I figured you for one of those skinny little Japanese monkeys, but you've changed my mind."

"Yo, brother. We'll throw you a heck of a welcome party if you join us, 'kay? We'd love to have a skilled navigator on board."

The one who spoke only in English piped up again. "Would you be interested in joining me for a movie?"

I couldn't understand what he said, so I didn't reply.

With Carol taking hold of my arm—or rather just hugging it at this point—I found myself completely surrounded by rough, strong REA members before I knew what was happening.

<Kessie, what do I do now?>

<Roger that, message received! It looks like you're in trouble, Zukky-san! Allow this pretty little fairy to guide you all forward!>

3

AS CAROL AND I ENTERED THE LOWER LEVELS OF THE dungeon, she was glued to my arm like we were a couple out on a date.

"Wait now, hold up boss," said one of REA's members, a burly Black man with a shotgun. "You can't be walking like that."

"Why not?" she replied. "Mizuki is a future party member of REA, and he's *mine* now. He's going to save us."

I don't recall when it was I became your property...or when I became a thing that could be owned, even.

But before I could say something to disagree, the shotgunner spoke first.

"That's fine, but what about our formation? It's going to be hard for you to move up, boss."

"I'll be fine," she said.

"*He* won't be. We should keep Mizuki just in front of the rear guard, sandwiched between him and our rear watch."

"He's safest by my side."

"I can't deny that, but let's do this the way we talked about in the meetings. Come on, boss. We're REA, aren't we? We aren't in London anymore."

Carol, reluctantly, gave me up to the guy with the shotgun.

"Sorry about her, Mizuki. The boss can get like this sometimes," he whispered in my ear as he led me away.

"Yeah... Carol's had a bit of a mood change, huh," I agreed. "What's wrong with her?"

"She can get like that when she finds something down in the dungeons she really likes. She starts fights with clients over things sometimes too. Once something strikes her fancy, she never wants to give it up."

"But why?" I asked.

"It's a long story. I know she's treating you like a possession right now, but she means well. She's just in that mode right now."

"Eh? What mode?"

"We don't know the particulars of it either, but I do have some guesses..."

Once we entered the lower levels, REA changed up its methods, just as Carol had indicated. The two assault team members at the front were moved one step backward, and our combat medic was added into the rear watch unit. Now that we were in the far more dangerous area, our formation included just one individual on the front line—Carol. She walked alone, carrying her western-style double-edged sword in the scabbard at her waist. Our formation, in numerical terms, had changed from a front line, rear guard, rear watch formation of 2-2-1 to a 1-2-2 formation down in the lower levels.

"Is she okay?" I asked of the shotgunner who just came back to serve as rear guard. I was still stuck between the rear guard and rear watch, which interfered with REA's formation a little.

"What do you mean?"

"I mean Carol, out there in front all alone. Isn't she in danger...?"

"Heh. Just watch," he said, grinning a little.

Then, it happened: we encountered our first monster in the lower levels, and my whole body froze up at the sight.

It was a tall demi-human, with reddened skin—an ogre. This monster was much bigger than any of the goblins were, with thick muscles on its legs and arms that surpassed anything a human could ever develop. It looked more like a gorilla than a man and had two small horns growing from its forehead. It carried a carved stone club in its hand.

I bet this thing could take down ten, no, twenty goblins just by swinging that club around.

"First time seeing an ogre?" asked the shotgunner, pointing his gun forward.

"Y-yeah..."

"They love human meat... And just like all the monsters down in the lower levels, they've got physical armor. Ogres have 4 points on average."

"Ah... Is that good?" I asked.

"It's a little high for the start of the lower levels. Converting rifle bullets into dungeon damage terms, they can cause 3 to 6 damage. We could still take him down with our guns, just barely, but we'd be using up a ton of ammunition to wear him down."

The Black man with the shotgun already seemed convinced that I was going to join REA. He was talking to me the way a senior at work might advise a newer hire—there was care in the way he spoke.

"You said we were like special forces earlier, didn't you?" he asked. "But the best that *we* can do is to run through those goblins on the upper levels. On the lower levels, we rely on Carol—she's the real boss of REA."

Carol slowly drew her sword from the scabbard at her waist. She faced her enemy, holding her weapon up at the midpoint between her shoulders—but instead of advancing on the ogre to strike it down, she stopped there in place, waiting.

"...Wh-what's she going to do?" I whispered to the shotgunner.

"In this situation, she won't make the first move. Right now she's using her Scale Eyes to analyze the ogre and figure out its stats."

Carol faced the ogre, motionless and calm, silently watching the monster while keeping a tight grip on her double-edged sword.

It was the ogre that blinked first. It watched her for a while, then swung its great club up onto one shoulder and lumbered straight towards her. Its giant feet pounded the rock below. Suddenly it broke into a charge and came at Carol, swinging wildly.

"Counter Flash," Carol muttered, and in the next instant, her blade was glowing. She stepped forwards, her small frame moving with explosive speed, as if that first step had brought her all the way up to full velocity. Her counterattack sliced at the ogre far faster than its club could find its target. Her blade traced its way up through the air and into the absurdly muscular chest of the monster, splitting it in two. A grotesque shower of dark purple blood splattered the cave.

Carol returned her sword to its scabbard, glanced once at the ogre she had just cut down to confirm it was dead, and then continued to walk forward as if nothing had happened.

As I stood there, stunned at what I'd just seen, the shotgunner nudged me in the shoulder.

"You see that, Mizuki? That's our boss. That there was her Sword Counter skill."

"Y-yeah... It really was awesome."

"Awesome doesn't do it justice, man," he went on as we followed her. "She's at level 40 at just sixteen years old... She was over 70 before the big shift happened." The shotgunner sounded so happy, as if he thought of her achievements as his own.

"We... Well, the boss and the rest of us at REA, y'see... We're going to be the best party of adventurers in the world! We'll overtake

Wallace Team in no time! The only thing Carol's lacking is age, that's all. She's still developing!"

"Hey... Do you mind if I ask you something?" I said.

"What is it?"

I moved in a little closer to the shotgunner and whispered, "How come Carol's so strong? And I mean, at such a young age too?"

"You don't know? Ah, I s'pose the boss hasn't told you," he replied in a whisper, looking surprised at the question. "She... Three years ago, Carol Middleton was caught up in the formation of the Dungeon of London. There were hundreds of other victims of that disaster. She was the only survivor."

4

WHAT FOLLOWS HERE IS AN ACCOUNT OF THAT story, based on information I received from multiple sources and some online articles.

Three years ago in the United Kingdom, thirteen-year-old Carol Middleton was living in London with her family. Her father and mother were both researchers at the University of London. She didn't have any incredible talents or noticeable abilities that made her stand out, but Carol was intelligent and composed for her age, and her family and neighbors all had high hopes for her future.

Then, late one night, the largest dungeon ever to form in the United Kingdom—the Dungeon of London—emerged within the city limits. The Middleton house, along with all the houses in their borough, were swallowed up in the event, and many residents woke in the middle of the night to find themselves already in the lower levels. The dungeon disaster that struck that night claimed over a thousand lives.

London police and emergency services were there immediately. A party of adventurers led by Wallace Chandler was dispatched from the United States at once to deal with the disaster and rescue those trapped inside the dungeon. Their search of the caves over the next few days was fruitless, however, and all they discovered were the corpses of the citizens of London, long since brutalized by the roaming monsters within.

It was on the third day, seventy-two hours after the dungeon had formed, that they found her—a young girl who had survived on the lower levels alone. She had been using a skill she happened upon to protect herself from the monsters, and she somehow managed to hold out for three whole days. When she was found, the girl was terribly weak, and she was rushed to an intensive care unit in a London-area hospital.

Strangely enough, she was discovered wearing several pieces of equipment on her person that seemed to be from the dungeon itself. The double-edged sword in her right hand seemed especially important to her, and she gripped it tightly even as her consciousness slipped—it couldn't be taken away from her.

For privacy reasons, it was only reported that a single survivor had been rescued from the dungeons. While her name was never officially released to the public, that young girl was none other than Carol Middleton.

"The plan was to finish with a survey of the lower levels today, but Mizuki's fine navigation has got us much further than we expected," Carol announced to the team once we'd made it some way down into the lower levels. "We have a real chance here—the kind that doesn't come around so often. Mizuki has been our MVP today, there's no doubt about that."

In my mind, the real MVP Kessie broke in with an *<Oh, you're too kind!>* as the fairy continued her frequent forays into my thoughts.

"As I result, I want to move on to locating and surveying a boss creature and taking it down if possible. As we discussed in our meetings, this dungeon clearing is to last just three days in total. This dungeon's not completely clear yet, but depending on scheduling things with the Omori City Police and JSDF, the next time we could get a proper shot at coming down here could be months or even a year into the future from now if we're unlucky."

"Let's go as far as we can get today, boss."

"Right. Any objections?"

Nobody seemed to have any.

I reached out to Kessie inside my head to—

<You called?!>

Well, I didn't call just yet. Man, that was a surprise. You're totally enjoying scaring me like this, aren't you?

I then spoke directly to her. *<So, this boss creature... Is it going be something like the dragon we met?>*

<Of course not, no way! If we met a dragon this close to the surface, it would kill us all in one second flat!>

<Then whatever we fight is going to be way weaker than a dragon. Gotcha.>

<Or, well, I suppose...> she began. *<The whole reason that dragon was on the upper levels is because something chased it up there, so maybe some of the upper-level monsters ran down here instead. I wonder how that will affect things?>*

<You mean it's possible the whole dungeon's difficulty level has been flipped upside-down?> I asked.

<Yep, yep.>

<Well, for starters, do you know where this boss creature is?> I asked.

<I sure do! I can already really feel how excited it is!>

My navigating (or Kessie's, rather) led Carol and the other REA members through the lower levels of the dungeon, and we proceeded largely unopposed. The Black man in charge of the rear watch, the shotgunner, seemed to still be in disbelief that I was capable of guiding them through the lower levels, areas I had never even been to before—but seeing how Carol looked somewhat excited at every new direction I gave, he seemed to have decided to hold his tongue.

<Oh? Hmm? Hm-hm?>

As we continued to follow Carol, and she went on cutting down every monster we encountered within ten seconds of laying eyes on it, Kessie's confused voice echoed through my head.

<What's the matter, Kessie?>

<Ahem... Uh... Wait a second, would you?>

She seemed to be in some trouble.

At the same time, Carol turned to look back at me with excitement and expectation in her eyes. "Mizuki, Mizuki. Another intersection. Which way do we go next?"

"Um... Just a minute." I pretended to think, reaching out to Kessie with my mind.

<Kessie? What's going on?> I asked.

<W-well, um...> she stammered. <The signals I was getting just completely cut off all of a sudden, see? I think we were getting pretty close, too...>

<So you can lose signal, eh?>

<I-I'm sorry... I might have just made a mistake...>

<It's fine, no worries,> I said, reassuring her. <You've done a great job just getting us this far. I'll do what I can to smooth this over with REA.>

Ding. My phone started vibrating, and I heard the incoming message sound. I reflexively took it out of my pocket, and looked down to see that I had several Lain messages from Shinobu—the very last one was a sticker.

I looked up at Carol, who was looking at me with a dubious expression on her face.

"What are you doing, Mizuki?"

"Ah, I'm sorry—I know we're at work. I just got a message."

"That's not what I meant," she said bluntly. "How do you have a signal?"

"...Huh?" I looked down at the phone in my hands—I completely took it for granted that I had a connection.

We're in the lower levels of a dungeon right now and my phone has a signal.

Wait... Didn't this happen with Shinobu's livestream too? We never figured out how she managed to stay connected, did we?

Suddenly, we heard a strange sound, like an electric current flowing.

Crackle.

Whatever Kessie had been tracking hadn't disappeared. Instead, it had changed form, became undetectable by her radar, and had snuck in close to us.

CHAPTER 9

MY FAIRY'S THE GREATEST IN THE WORLD

1

NONE OF US NOTICED THE THING APPROACH.

On hearing a dull sound like an electric current, Carol spun around and drew her sword in one swift motion. With supernatural reflexes, she parried the oncoming lightning bolt and the electric attack slid off her blade. The attacks kept coming though, only speeding up as she tried to push them back—a bolt split in two, reflected off the blade of her sword, and launched toward the two REA members behind her.

"Gah!!!"

"Ahh?!"

Their bodies shook fiercely, and there was another crack as a strong current ran through them, as if a great piece of rubber suddenly snapped and its tension released. The shotgunner turned his weapon towards one of the three branching paths before us and began unloading. Our combat medic, the one without an Auto-Translate skill, started to run over to one of the shocked rear guards... but the moment he moved, the lightning came again, taking him from an unexpected angle.

"WHA?!?!" he yelled in mangled English.

A high-voltage current burst towards him from the stone walls of the cave, and the combat medic was scorched by the lightning attack.

<Zukky-san! Get down! It's dangerous!>

I took my pistol out from its holster on my right thigh and instinctively rolled to the ground. I heard Kessie's voice in my brain, not through my ears, which let me react faster than usual. In that same moment, another lightning attack shot out from the cave's stone walls. It passed right over the spot where I had been standing just moments ago and landed a direct hit on the back of the shotgunner. He went rigid, shotgun still in hand. He let out an awful cry as his body trembled.

I still couldn't grasp the situation. I hadn't taken it all in—but what the shotgunner's fall meant was that every member of our party except Carol and myself had been taken out of action in an instant.

"Carol!" I screamed.

It was a reflex on my part—perhaps there was no reason to be screaming her name. She didn't answer me anyway. She lowered her center of gravity and turned the point of her sword to the ground, taking a somewhat looser stance. Carol didn't even spare a glance at her teammates lying on the ground around her. There were no words of concern, no signs of panic—she was completely composed. It looked to me less like cold-hearted insensitivity and more a testament to the absolute responsibility she felt. She had to handle the situation now that she was the only one left.

All her attention was focused on the middle path of the three that branched out before her. I heard a little crackling sound from one of the rock faces behind her.

"Behind you! To the left!" I called out.

A moment after I heard the noise, a lightning attack jumped from the rock and headed towards Carol. She turned the top half of her body towards the current and managed to parry it with her blade again, as if she had known it was coming. She was an expert in her techniques and so incredibly quick that it was like watching a video being fast-forwarded and dropping half the frames. She had movements the human eye simply couldn't follow. Her incredibly high Agility stat made these superhumanly fast reflexes possible.

The current she blocked bounced away behind her and dispersed harmlessly against the rock walls, losing its strength. The moment after she parried the attack, her eyes returned back to the paths. She resumed her stance.

For a time, then, there was silence. I lay there with my pistol in my hand, though unsure why, holding my breath and watching her intently. I had no idea why I was safe when the others had fallen.

<Stay perfectly still! Don't move, I mean it!> Kessie's voice echoed inside my head.

And so I waited, silently frozen there in the tense cave, not even lifting a finger.

At last, I heard footsteps stomping down the dark path Carol's eyes were trained upon. The thing slowly emerged from the darkness, illuminated by the light of one of the fallen assault rifles.

This monster was dark and had abnormally large shoulders, thick limbs, and an insanely muscular build. Its canine teeth were unusually long. And in its hand it held a big club carved of stone— too big for my liking.

That's an ogre, I thought, *but there's something different about this one, it's not like the others we've encountered.*

There were yellow hues to the creature's skin, and there were two horns sprouting from its forehead, much larger and longer than any of the others we had faced. Its long white hair dangled from its scalp and covered its back. The tips of the strands floated a little, as if they were filled with static electricity.

This one's clearly a higher level than all the other ones we've faced... And these features... I think maybe a Japanese guy like me would recognize it better than a Brit like Carol. This yellow ogre looks like an oni to me, like from Japanese folklore.

Carol lowered herself closer to the ground. Her arms and shoulders were completely relaxed, and it looked as if the only strength she was exerting was what little it took to curl her fingers around the hilt of her double-edged sword to keep it from falling from her hands.

There was tension there too—I had no idea when the point of her sword might suddenly and violently flick upward. Carol was as ready as could be to react to her enemy at a moment's notice. The yellow-skinned ogre faced off against Carol, and for a moment just glared at her, unmoving. Carol was motionless as well, and after a few moments of silence, she spoke.

"...Physical armor 20, Magic armor 30, HP 15... You get that, Mizuki?" Carol muttered the information to me without turning her head, and she slowly raised her sword up to shift into an offensive stance.

"...Huh?" I managed to say.

"That's the intel. Now run."

"Wait, Carol—!"

The moment I screamed, the ogre raised his hand, and an electric current flowed forth. Carol parried and charged at the ogre so fast she seemed to be flying towards it. In the narrow passageway, she switched the grip on her sword to thrust its point at the monster and shot towards the ogre like a bullet. She moved with such explosive speed it was as if all the energy she had been building up had just been fired off all at once.

"Goblin Assault! Demolishing Strike! Damage Duplication!"

Carol activated several different skills as she charged at the ogre, but just before the tip of her sword made contact, the walls around it jumped to life all at once. Bright sparks electrified the air. It was as if the monster had been expecting her.

"Tch." Carol clicked her tongue.

Illuminated by the glow of the lightning, she seemed to have realized something. The moment before her blade sank into the ogre's body, the furious flash of another electric attack filled the passageway. The shocks seemed to come at her from all directions and swallowed her whole. The high voltage current passed into her thin frame and seemed like it was going to burn her to ashes.

"Ah! Ngh! Kyaaaah!!!"

Her violent screaming echoed through the cave. Her body trembled and twitched as she slumped to her knees.

"Nn, ngh... Ahh..."

Carol let out another weak cry and collapsed to the ground. Even after falling, she continued to twitch like a fish on dry land... Perhaps it was due to the current still lingering in her small body.

The ogre looked down at her, crouched, and grabbed at her long hair.

"Aahh...!"

The yellow ogre held her up by her helmet and hair and looked at her intently, as if inspecting her beautiful face.

"Nnh... Ah..."

The ogre silently reached in through a gap in her armor, and his hand closed over her bare wrist. Then, once more, another strong current ran through her body—delivered directly this time.

Carol screamed loudly. "Nngh! Aah! Aaahhh!!!"

Damn it!!!

I stood up and prepared to shoot the monster, pointing my pistol towards the ogre as it tormented Carol. Kessie seemed to read my movements though, and her high-pitched voice reverberated in my head, urging me to wait.

<Hold on! Stop! Stoooooop!!!> she yelled.

<But Kessie! We can't let this go on!>

<Even so—! You can't! You can't, you can't, you can't! It seriously super-duper isn't possible!!! No no no!!!>

<Then what am I supposed to do?!>

<Just wait a minute!> she told me. *<Stay! Wait it out a while!!! Don't move!!!>*

<But we have to!>

<Nope! Wait! Calm it! Calm down! Calm down calm down—! You aren't going up against that superior enemy with no plan and nothing to fight it with! Nothing good comes of unplanned actions! Now stop moving, I mean it!!!>

2

"N H... UGH...! UHHH..."

Carol, tormented by the direct electric shocks to her body, was flat on the floor of the dungeon. Drool dripped from the corner of her mouth. She seized up from the current left inside her, letting out pained moans with every occasional spasm.

Her long golden hair was splayed out across the ground, and her pale cheek pressed against the gravel was wet with heavy and unending tears from the sharp pain.

<That's a boss ogre! An electric variant at that!> Kessie's voice was now a permanent telepathic resident in my head, urging me not to make any sudden moves.

<A regular old boss ogre wouldn't be all that rare a sight around here! But if there's a super high-level variant like that guy walking around? Wahh!!! I was wrong about what I said earlier! It might really be true...!>

<What is it, Kessie?! What's going on? Calm down!>

<Just like with that dragon earlier, yeah?! Maybe the whole difficulty level of this dungeon is topsy-turvy! All the guys that are supposed to be in the depths are hanging out on upper levels! These bosses have lost their places and are all just wandering around!!!>

<What in the world?! That's terrible!> I yelled back. <So it's like starting up an RPG and facing the last boss in the tutorial village, and all his elites in the next village over?!>

<Aaand this thing has 20 physical armor and 30 magic armor! That sure is one thick ogre! We're lucky he's got low HP like most of his kind, but attacks won't even get through to him! Ah, curses! He's too tough!!! His attack patterns are super strong too! What do we doooo?!>

I played dead and continued my internal screaming match with Kessie. The only reason we were able to talk with any degree of calm at all was because the ogre had decided not to kill Carol outright. Having shocked her into paralysis with excessive attacks, he began to play with her.

"Nnh... Gah..."

The ogre stripped off the armor she was wearing, piece by piece.

When it came across parts that seemed difficult to unfasten, he just pulled at them until they broke.

Rip! I could hear the sound of tearing clothes. I heard her white gambeson being torn off along her back, as if the monster was removing the clothes from a doll.

The ogre was interested in her flesh, and with the effects of the electric attacks still running through her body, Carol could do nothing to resist him. She summoned all her strength and tried to tighten her grip on the double-edged sword in her right hand—but the ogre pried her fingers from it and threw the blade far away across the cave. He then flipped her over onto her back and peeled the white fabric from her.

"Nn... Nhhh...!" she moaned again.

With her upper garments torn away, Carol's small breasts were now exposed.

I averted my eyes and cursed inside my head. *Damn it. What do we do...?*

<Kessie... Why isn't that thing attacking me?> I asked.

<I-It's because you're playing dead...>

<That's really what's fooling it?>

<I-I think so, yep. That monster is a little different in how it detects its surroundings... It doesn't react to things that don't move. Look at its eyes. See?>

I looked up at the boss ogre's eyes at her insistence. Sure enough, his pupils were glazed over, completely clouded with gray. There were flashing electromagnetic wave-like blocks of electricity spaced out evenly on the stone walls around him.

<I think those are the things he uses to fire off those lightning attacks... They also act like a kind of radar. They're set up around the dungeon...> she said.

How it worked wasn't clear, but it seemed like those items were spread out and connected wirelessly, probably letting him detect things from far away. It also looked like he could use them for attacks.

<Is that how he knew we were coming, maybe...?>

<I think so, yes...>

I supposed that explained why I suddenly got a phone signal again. *That ogre's been setting up signal tower-like things down here in the dungeon to communicate... And then whenever there's an unfamiliar movement from an intruder into his field, that gets passed back to him, through a series of signal stations, I guess... And that just happens to also allow phones to connect to it too...?*

<I-I've got no idea what you're saying...> Kessie said, reading my thoughts.

<Don't worry. I'm confusing myself just thinking about it too. I don't understand this either.>

I wasn't much for science, so I didn't know the details of the process. At best, I was trying to connect what I could see to the dubious scientific knowledge I *did* possess.

<Well, anyway... That's kind of what I figure is happening.>

As Kessie and I continued our telepathic conversation, Carol's crisis continued to unfold in the present. With her unable to do anything to get away, the ogre had stripped off almost all of her upper gear. Only the metal part of her gauntlets connected to her palms remained. Her small, rounded shoulders, both of her breasts, and everything else down to her belly button that should have been covered up was instead laid bare.

The ogre looked at her, licked his lips, and flipped her over again onto her front. He now put his hands around her backside and began to prod at the gear protecting her lower body.

"Ah... H-huh... Nh!"

I heard her let out a dry, hoarse moan. She was about to be defiled by the ogre, a creature whose raw strength she could not hope to contend with, even in her wildest dreams. The monster was two times taller than her. It had stripped her naked, pushed her down helplessly, and was now forcing its raw, animal desires upon her.

I can't even imagine how scared she must be.

The ogre began to use his thick fingers to pull off the armor at her waist.

"S... Sto...p... Nnh!" she cried out quietly, tears streaming down her face.

The ogre's hands could easily bend metal plate, and the creature panted with excitement as he ran his hands over her rear.

<Th-this isn't good... I've gotta do something! We're getting into dangerous territory!>

<Uuumm... P-protect your life!> Kessie yelled in my head. *<Can't we just do that...? Ah ahem, you see... I do feel really, reaaally bad for Carol-san, but we should just play dead and wait this out...>*

<Nope. Can't do that.>

<But like, that thing has 20 physical armor, you know? Unless your attacks deal over 20 damage, it'll be like they never even happened...! The thing has 30 whole magical armor as well, see? The only spell you've got is Blaze, and that deals 4 damage, Zukky-san...>

I thought for a moment. *<I can use that Chip Damage skill Heath gave me. That deals true damage, it'll be able to get through. I'll use Skillbook to activate it, then attack the ogre with my pistol...>*

<...It's got 15 HP.> Kessie reminded me. *<Can you hit that ogre fifteen times?>*

I was quiet at that.

<Not to mention he isn't just going to stand there and let you, you know. He could take you out in a single blow, and you'd have to land

fifteen hits to take him down. Can you really hit him with that pistol thing...?>

...*Nope*, I thought. *That's definitely not happening...*

It was probably impossible. Especially with the Colt Government I had in my hands, anyway.

I figured that with my technique, just managing to hit the ogre once would take all I had. *Even if it doesn't come attack me, reloading this pistol in between those fifteen shots doesn't seem worth the attempt. It's like saying, "Oh yeah, you can defeat this boss if you just land fifteen critical hits on it." It's just not gonna happen!*

I shifted my gaze to another weapon lying on the ground. The closest one to me, within reach if I lunged for it, was an assault rifle.

How many bullets are in that thing? Even if I spotted an opening and grabbed it, am I even going to be able to shoot it? I mean, I'd also need to turn Chip Damage into a card and then activate it...right?

"K-kill me..."

I heard Carol's hoarse cries from across the cave and turned my eyes to her. She was lying face down on the floor. The clothes and gear on her upper body had been long since torn off, revealing her smooth skin and the muscles of her back, slender like a cat's. The armor on her arms and legs still remained.

Crack!

The sound was another of the metal fittings on her armor being forcefully snapped in two. The ogre lifted her up by her waist and removed another piece of gear from her smooth, curved, protruding backside. All protection there was now gone, and the only thing separating her lower body from the air was light clothing she wore under the metal.

Under that, there's probably just her underwear. And if she isn't wearing any today, then... No, she's gotta be wearing underwear... But either way, that'll be the point when I stop buying time and do something. What comes after that is nothing but the awful act itself, the kind of thing you only find in certain thin, age-restricted comics that are in terrible taste. I have to get moving before that ogre gets it on. If fifteen hits dealing 1 damage each won't cut it... What about one hit that deals 35 damage, powering through his 20 physical armor and 15 HP?

<We wouldn't be having so much trouble if you did have a way to deal that much damage in one hit...> Kessie said.

<Of course not. I was being an idiot.>

I paused. *Hold on. Wait a minute...*

I went over my skills once more.

BLAZE
Rank E Level 7 Required
Magical Attack
Deal 4 points fire damage to target.
Damage over time: 3 (burning)

CHIP DAMAGE
Rank A - Level 25 Required
Buff Skill
All attacks deal 1 additional point of attack damage.
This additional damage cannot be prevented.

GOBLIN ASSAULT
Rank D - Level 15 Required
Buff Skill
For 1 turn, all your melee range physical attacks deal
    +3 additional damage.

Of those three, Blaze was the only one I had carded. Chip Damage and Goblin Assault weren't carded yet, and at Level 19, I didn't even have the required level for one of them.

Then, there was Skillbook itself... There was still a lot I didn't know about it. It seemed like skills that were turned into cards had ten uses, and they could be activated regardless of their required level... But I still needed to place the skill cards into the binder each time I wanted to activate them.

I thought this all over.

<Zukky-san, you aren't thinking about doing anything dangerous, are you?>

<Maybe,> I told Kessie telepathically. *<I mean... If I really risked everything, then...I might be able to target his technique's weak spot to do something really crazy.>*

<...I don't feel like trying, to be honest,> she said.

Well, I suppose it is like risking your life on something you aren't even sure is there... I thought. *But I can't be sure this won't work either. It might fail...but it might not.*

<Kessie, can you talk to Carol telepathically?>

<I could, but... Are you sure about this?>

<Just connect to her... I'll leave the explaining up to you.>

I felt Kessie's presence disappear from my mind, and float over to Carol's.

I returned to planning my next move. *Right, then... As for this buggy maneuver, I've only ever thought about doing it once before. The time I mentioned it to Kessie, she said it would be totally hilarious if I managed to pull it off.*

A finishing move using Skillbook... Should I go ahead and give it a try?

3

Just as the ogre was stripping off her underwear, Carol started to hear Kessie's voice inside her head. There was a look of surprise on her face when it happened. With eyes that were wet and puffy from crying, she looked over at me on the floor.

Ten seconds later, Kessie's consciousness was back inside my head.

<I went and explained everything to her!>

<Did she understand?>

<I think for now, sure! She was surprised, but she was more focused on accepting the situation than asking questions!> Kessie then paused. *<Oh, also! I asked if she could move, and she said could, a little bit!>*

<Really?> I asked.

<It seems like she was waiting for an opening of her own to strike back at that thing. She said it's been a bit of time since the first attack, so she's recovered a little!>

<All right. If that's the case, then...>

Kessie acted as a go-between for Carol and me so we could go over the basics of our strategy.

We've only got one chance, and there's plenty of cause for concern here...

That said, after talking to Carol, we came up with a plan that was sure to succeed if everything went well—my "not even sure if this will work" idea (or gamble, really) was shelved as a Plan B.

I activated Skillbook and made the card binder appear beside my face.

"Two skills have not yet been carded. Card skills?"

I was going to turn both of them into cards, but I couldn't press the "Yes" button just yet. *I have to make my move when the time is right.*

Carol pretended to be completely wiped out. She didn't move a single finger and let the ogre do as he liked with her body—but her blue eyes were fixed on me.

What is she feeling right now? What emotions lie behind those eyes? I'm sorry for hanging back this long. But if I can pull this off... forgive me at least a little bit, won't you?

Finally Carol's underwear was lowered all the way, and her soft, perky bottom was exposed. It was plump and youthfully round, tight with just the right amount of muscle.

"...!" Even with the moment of truth fast approaching, Carol's face flushed with shame at having her butt completely on display.

Nothing we can do about that now. Please endure it a little longer.

The ogre tried to tear her panties off her legs, but they got caught on her thighs and seemed to cause him some trouble. The fabric then got caught on the armor pieces still attached to her legs, and he couldn't get them off. The ogre seemed to get frustrated by this and grabbed her underwear on both sides, trying to force it off. I heard a ripping sound, and the cloth stretched out as far as it would go...

Finally, the white panties ripped apart in the ogre's hands.

Then, it happened, at the exact moment the ogre completely tore her panties from her thighs. In that instant, she was completely free from the monster's rough hands.

"Yaaah!!!"

Carol suddenly pushed herself up from the floor with all her strength and sprang upright. With most of her armor, all of her clothes, and now even her underwear ripped away, her naked form flew through the air with only the bits that really didn't need hiding still covered up. The weight of the armor on her limbs gave her the centrifugal force to launch into a powerful spin, rotating her light body through the air.

In that instant, I saw everything between her legs as well. It's not like I was interested in what she had down there, but I began to regret that my eyes didn't have any recording capabilities or slow-motion playback—for other, unrelated reasons, of course.

<I can hear all this!!!> Kessie reminded me.

Carol's leap into the air ended in a full force spinning kick, and her foot landed squarely on the ogre's jaw.

"Chip Damage!" she cried out.

The skill was worth 200,000 yen on the market and had been gaining popularity among top-class adventurers for years—of course Carol had it too.

Chip Damage's true damage goes through physical armor, so her kick just dealt that thing 1 point.

The ogre stumbled from the sudden attack, and he fell backwards from the sharp impact of the kick to his jaw.

14 more to go.

In that same moment, I opened my Skillbook and quickly tapped to turn my own Chip Damage and Goblin Assault skills into cards. The two cards appeared in the air before me, floating there and waiting for me to take them.

So this is how it works! I had never turned a skill into a card before, but I had run through a few ideas in my head of what the process might look like.

The worst-case scenario would have been if the card had teleported itself somewhere into the Skillbook and I had to spend time flipping through to find it... But whatever, I'm just glad that didn't happen!

As I picked myself up from the ground, I grabbed both cards and loaded them into slots in the book.

It worked! I did it just as fast as I did all those times I practiced in my head!

The moment the cards were in the binder, I drew one of them.

"Chip Damage!"

I used Skillbook to activate Chip Damage and gained a +1 true damage buff to my attacks. A display opened up on the left side of my vision and showed an hourglass-like gauge, counting down.

So this is how skill durations are displayed!

I mentally confirmed the way that Skillbook worked as the life-or-death battle unfolded before me. I put the card I just drew back into the binder and pulled out my pistol.

There's one more thing I actually want to check out... But there's no time for that now! I have to get this over as quickly as possible, just like we discussed!

I swiftly but calmly pointed the muzzle of my Government straight at the ogre.

Carol, through Kessie, had told me what to do. <*Stay calm, turn off the safety, and hold on tight to the grip.*>

I did as she told me.

"Aaaahh!!!" I cried.

I gripped the Colt Government with all my might and wildly pulled the trigger. The sharp sounds of gunfire echoing off the walls of the narrow cave made my eardrums rattle, causing a sharp ringing in my ears.

Carol, who had just dealt the surprise blow that sent the ogre reeling to the ground, ducked low to let my bullets pass over her.

Just as we discussed. So far, everything's going according to plan.

*This Government has seven and one bullets loaded into it...I think.
I wasn't the last one to load it, so I'm not sure.*

I fired off all the bullets I had at the ogre, but I had no idea how
many of them made contact. The recoil was much stronger than I
expected, and even I could tell that my aim had drifted up and to
the right.

"Mizuki! Just 13 points left!" Carol screamed. She had analyzed
the ogre's stats with her Scale Eyes.

*If this thing started at 15 HP...and Carol and I dealt it 2 damage...
then only one of my shots actually hit him! No point in cursing my awful
aim now through—I'm lucky to have even hit that monster once!*

I forced my empty Government back into its holster with the
slide still pulled back. I rolled across the ground towards the nearby
assault rifle.

*This is the real deal! Carol says there are thirty bullets in this thing,
so I just need to shoot like crazy and hit my target a third of the time!*

<Zukky-san!!!>

I heard Kessie's voice, followed by a crackling sound that indicated an incoming lightning attack.

No! I can't dodge it!

"Yaaaah! Haaah!!!"

Yelling out, Carol leaped up from where she'd been lying at the
ogre's feet and launched herself at the yellow-skinned monster. Both
of her legs landed on the ogre's shoulders, and she slid her bare thighs
so she could tighten them around the ogre's neck. She used the armor
on her legs and arms to swing her crotch around to its face and lock
down the monster's vision, using the weight of her remaining gear to
her advantage. Then, with her core strength, she quickly folded her
body around the ogre, spinning around him and tossing him with
such force I thought his neck could break from the momentum.

That was a murderous in-air technique that would put a luchador to shame! What do you mean, you can move a "little"?! Those are some amazing athletic abilities! She's making me kind of jealous!

"Chip Damage!" she called out.

The ogre collided with the ground headfirst. The electric attack that had been coming straight for me curved in the air, landing a direct hit on the assault rifle I had been reaching for instead, blowing it across the cave.

I'm not sure if that counted...but that was probably another point of damage! Twelve to go!

"Eek! Aaahh!"

Carol tried to make a clean landing after her toss, but she was caught in midair by the ogre's electric attacks. She missed her footing and fell to the ground. It seemed like that really used the last of her strength—Carol remained completely silent and motionless where she landed.

The assault rifle I had gone for was now smoldering and smoking. I started to look around for another firearm, but I heard the sounds of several more electric attacks being prepared before I could move.

"Whoaaa?!"

But they weren't aimed at me. Instead, they struck all the weapons on the ground around me, turning my last hopes to dust.

Damn it!

The ogre stood up, glaring over at me and steadying his aim as he did.

All I've got left is this empty pistol and the three magazines at my waist. But those electric attacks he's been firing off left and right do seem to be tiring him out!

I've got just a little leeway now, my Skillbook, and my empty Colt Government.

He's got 12 HP left!

There's nothing else to do. It's time for a gamble—time for Plan B!

4

I OPENED UP MY BINDER AND DREW A DIFFERENT CARD. "Goblin Assault!"

The card I activated this time was Goblin Assault—a buff skill that added +3 physical damage to close combat attacks. A new timer appeared on the left side of my field of vision that showed the duration of the new buff. I quickly put the card back into the binder and immediately pulled it out again.

"Goblin Assault!"

The skill activated once more, and a new timer appeared next to the first one. The time didn't increase or cancel out the first one—instead, it added a new timer right next to the original one, indicating the second instance seemed to stack with the first.

Meaning that right now, in total, I've got +6 to physical damage up close!

All right! I knew it!!!

When cast normally, Goblin Assault had a cooldown between uses. The length of the cooldown was a few seconds longer than the length of the buff's effect, meaning that under normal circumstances, the ability could never be stacked. *But what about if I activate it using Skillbook?* I thought. *Maybe the cooldown of Goblin Assault is cancelled out by putting the skill card back into my binder... meaning I could stack the buff on myself multiple times?*

That was my simple prediction about the system—and it paid off brilliantly.

This Skillbook lets me stack the effects of skills on top of each other that were never intended to be stackable! It's like a backdoor kind of trick in a game—something the developers didn't predict!

The ogre stood back up.

How much longer before that monster can attack again?!

I went on activating Goblin Assault repeatedly. *I've got to stack this until it won't stack any longer! To the limit!*

"Goblin Assault! Goblin Assault! Goblin Assault! Goblin Assault! Goblin Assault! Gob— Go—, Go-go—! Goblin Assault!"

I stuttered! Do I even need to say the name of the skill every time? How many more until it's maxed out?!

I looked down at the remaining uses on the card—*just two left!*

I could hear the sound of electric attacks building around me.

No! I'm not going to make it!!

Suddenly, flashes of gunfire ripped through the dungeon, and the booming sound of bullets filled the air.

"Fxxk!" someone yelled in English. "My arse!! PLEASE!!!"

I've got no idea what that guy's saying!!!

The REA combat medic, the man who so often showered me with English phrases I couldn't understand, was lying on the ground with his sidearm pistol drawn. He was firing wildly at the boss ogre. Perhaps it was his fighting spirit kicking in as he clearly hadn't recovered completely—only his head was turned toward the ogre, and he aimed with one hand as he fired. It didn't seem like he had any buffs applied though, so while several of his shots *did* hit the boss ogre, the monster showed no sign that it was being damaged. They did seem to displease him though, and the charges the ogre had been saving up were directed at the combat medic instead.

"Jesus!!!" he yelled.

I've made it now! Just in the nick of time, thanks to that guy who really needs to buy himself an Auto-Translate skill! I never have any clue what he's saying, but he taunted the boss. That moment he bought me was just enough to get two more stacks of this skill out!

"Goblin Assault! Goblin Assault!"

There were now ten gauges counting down in the corner of my vision. The first one was just about to run out, but the duration of Chip Damage seemed to be a bit on the long side, so it was still holding out.

The ogre finally turned to me.

To be honest, I also want to get a stack of Chip Damage in... But I'm at my limit.

I steeled myself and charged at the yellow-skinned monster. I leaped into the air and readied a dropkick. The ogre saw me coming and raised it arms to counter me, readying its electric attacks.

Everything happened almost simultaneously.

Goblin Assault's +3 damage times 10 would do 30 damage.

And Chip Damage is +1 damage.

That makes 31 damage!!!

"Yaaahh!!!"

The moment before my kick landed—the one I put every last drop of my strength into—there was a spark, a *crack!* And a shock of electric current shot through my body.

I lost all strength, and in midair, my form faltered...but my leg, splayed out in front of me, somehow managed to just barely scrape against the ogre's breastplate.

With a force reminiscent of an explosion, the two of us were blown apart from each other. It was a force that no normal dropkick could ever produce, and it was more like being caught up in the blast of a powerful bomb.

I was blown backwards, but the ogre, perhaps because of the way I just grazed him, was blown backwards and down into the ground, cracking into the hard stone walls of the dungeon. The way the monster flew was so unrealistic it reminded me of a physics engine bug from a video game.

What happened...?! Did that little graze from my foot count as one damage?! If my kick dealt 0 damage, then the total would come to 31... I needed to cause 32 damage to overcome his 20 physical armor and 12 HP... If so, I was 1 damage short!

I fell backwards and my back skidded and scraped against the rock below me. The impact was so strong I kept sliding. I looked over to the ogre as I did...and I saw the monster already trying to get back up, stumbling for footing.

I was a point short after all!

I immediately pulled my Government out of its holster and took a magazine from my left hip.

How do I get rid of the empty one...? Aha, here's the button!

I pressed it hard with my thumb to eject the empty magazine, and remembering the lecture that Carol had given me, pushed the new one into place.

You practiced this so many times in your head! Get in there!

With trembling hands, I struck the magazine and it slid into place—so roughly I thought it might break. With bullets reloaded and the hammer still down, I gripped the pistol tightly and I pointed it towards the ogre...

And at that exact moment, Chip Damage's duration ran out.

I shuddered, my pistol still pointing straight at the monster.

Damn it! I was so focused on reloading I didn't check the timers!!!

The ogre stood back up and turned its hand towards me.

Even if I landed all my shots, I won't get through that thing's physical armor! I'm just one point of damage short, but I don't have time to open up Skillbook and reactivate Chip Damage now...!

"Zukky-san!" Kessie screamed out loud.

I didn't know what she wanted to say at that moment, but I moved on instinct.

"Skillbook!"

I made the thick card binder appear above my head, and in the same instant, Kessie shot out of my vest pocket. She flew straight at the falling book, its pages flapping open as it dropped to the ground.

"Kessie!"

"Roger that!"

As the book continued its free fall, Kessie immediately found the skill card as the pages fluttered. Flying directly above the book she managed to draw it out from the binder. It was a miracle.

You're the greatest fairy in the world, no question! Well, I figure maybe you're the only fairy in the world...

Either way, the card she drew from the binder was, of course, *that one*. And all the conditions were met.

"Chip Damage!"

A new hourglass appeared in the left corner of my vision— I tightened my grip on the Government and shot like hell. Of the seven bullets I haphazardly shot towards the ogre, most seemed to pass under its arms—but I kept pulling the trigger. Finally, once the pistol was spent and the last of the used shell casings were out, the Government fell silent in my hands, its purpose fulfilled.

The cave was quiet.

I was still flat on my back with an empty pistol pointed at the monster. The ogre just stood there in silence.

Did I get a hit in? Did I miss all those shots?

Just as the chilling thoughts began to form in the back of my mind...

"Guh..."

The yellow-skinned giant collapsed to the ground with a great *thud*.

One of my .45 ACP bullets had, miraculously, made contact—dealing 1 true damage to the ogre and eliminating its last hit point.

Even a terrible shot can hit their target with enough tries.

I dropped my Government, laid on the ground, and sighed. "Ah... I beat it..."

Boss ogre, taken out.

It was thus that my first real dungeon clearing ended in an unbelievable surprise victory.

CHAPTER 10

THERE'S AN EXTREMELY HIGH CHANCE SHE'S HIS DAUGHTER

1

AFTER WE DEFEATED THE BOSS OGRE, WE WAITED A while for everyone to recover. Then, we safely made our way back to the entrance of the Omori Dungeon. All of Carol's clothes had been torn off, so the combat medic had given her his to wear. He himself was now nearly naked, only in his underpants, vest, and combat gear. He was making an incredibly masculine exit from the mission.

The loot from our trip was a magic spell named "Signal Relay" from the boss ogre, and a skill called "Physical Armor" that had dropped from one of the regular ogres.

Then, there was a Blessing of Eir, which we found up one of the three branching paths. It was inside a treasure chest in a corner of the cave the boss ogre seemed to have made its home. When I first found the thing, I couldn't believe my eyes. Records were that only one had ever been discovered, after all—it was an item of legend, but we seemed to just kind of stumble upon it.

With that one discovery, our primary mission goal was complete. Even I, with my lack of dungeoneering experience, could tell that.

"It's weird," said Carol. The young woman was wearing a man's shirt, and her thin hands were peeking out from their loose sleeves. Her baggy trousers were only held in place by a tight belt at her waist. "What's an item like a Blessing of Eir doing in a place like this?"

"So they *can* just be lying around like that, huh? Lucky break, isn't it?" I asked lightly.

The burly shotgunner had been brought back to consciousness after all those electric attacks, and he gave me a bit of an eye roll. "Mizuki, it's like this," he started. "Imagine you want to become a billionaire, so you go out and buy a lottery ticket, and just happen to hit the jackpot, yeah?"

"What are you saying?"

"I'm *saying* that clearly something weird is going on."

I don't really get the way these foreigners are framing this...

In any case, it seemed that I was the only one present willing to write our discovery off as just good luck. Carol and her team members talked among themselves as they looked at the magic item with skeptical eyes.

"We should get an appraiser to check if this thing's real."

"We can leave that to Horinomiya, yeah? The thing's his now, either way."

"What if it *is* the real deal?"

"Maybe we need to talk about this."

"I'd actually be way more comfortable if this thing was just a replica."

The English-speaking one seemed excited. "This has got me so hot and bothered."

I watched the professional adventurers continue their discussion in words I could and couldn't understand. I reached out to Kessie in my mind.

<Hey Kessie. Do coincidences like these just happen down here in the dungeons?>

<How should I put this... I don't really understand what you're all so surprised about, personally.>

<How come?>

<Well, I mean... Blessings of Eir are pretty standard items in my world. If I had to say more... Then I guess they are a little bit rare... But they aren't like, treasures on a super-extra amazing level or anything,> she explained.

<They aren't?>

<Nope... At least not really. Anyway, it could be that the people in this world just aren't high enough levels at the moment, so they aren't properly exploring the dungeons,> she said. <That would explain this little monster mix-up and that item that should be a little bit deeper in the dungeon... It might be why you're all so excited?>

<So this item isn't much of a surprise to you?>

<It would be like in that DVD we watched the other day, Dragon Quist, if someone was really, really surprised to find a nice potion and treated it like some legendary item, I guess?>

I see. Maybe these dungeon things are far vaster than we think they are. Or like... Thinking about it from this other world's perspective... Maybe it looks like humanity is just paddling around, playing in the shallows, when there's a whole ocean out there.

The Blessing of Eir was a cure-all, a medicine for all ills. If it was possible to get those in the "shallow waters" of a dungeon and they aren't even all that rare... I could only wonder what items were sleeping all the way down in the depths of these caves.

In any case, we left the dungeon. Horinomiya was surprised when he saw our wounds and the way Carol was dressed, but he was even more shocked to learn of the results of our exploration.

"You... You've really found it, then?" he asked.

"It's hard for us to believe this too," said Carol. "I recommend you wait, for now, until an appraiser can accurately confirm this to be a genuine item."

"Yes, I will. Ah, but... To think you would truly find it..." Horinomiya held the crystal shaped item in both hands with great care. His body was shaking a little, perhaps because of the built-up nerves of many years searching for his prize.

"I-I'm quite happy to call this mission accomplished. You've achieved the end goal I set out, after all."

"Then, as stipulated in the contract, I expect the full reward to be deposited into our account by next week," said Carol. "I will once more caution you against refusing to send payment."

"Of course," replied Horinomiya. "I wouldn't dream of it."

Carol, perhaps remembering our earlier discussion, then looked at him sharply. "If on the off chance we *are* given insufficient compensation...we will be absolutely sure to collect, making full use of the information we gathered in advance—whether that should lead to your bankruptcy or not. Please do not forget that."

"...I know, all right? Thank you."

With that, Carol looked over to me. "For now, I've given him a basic warning. If this man doesn't pay you properly, there's nothing to fear. REA will handle it. Just say the word."

"Okay," I said. "Hey, thanks."

"Ah..."

"Um..."

A sudden silence fell over us. There was so much we needed to talk about and go over together... There was a mountain of things we needed to apologize for, but neither of us knew where to start.

"Anyway," Carol broke the silence. "There are still many issues to deal with that involve you too. We'll be staying in Japan for a while longer to investigate this dungeon. Let's talk again later."

"Sure. I'm ready to turn in for the day."

"Mizuki." She called my name again. "Let me just say this, at the very least... A lot happened down there, but ultimately, you saved me. Thank you."

"Ah, right. I...I still don't really know how to say this..." I started.

"...It doesn't seem like we're going to get a handle on this conversation today. Some other time." She then smirked and made to walk away in her baggy shirt and trousers. "See you around."

"Yeah. See you around."

After all the post-dungeon weapon storage and various rounds of paperwork were done, the members of REA and I went our separate ways. It was quite a hard day's work, but the reward...

Come to think of it, I'm set to get several hundreds of million yen for successfully completing this mission.

The thought made the whole thing feel a little unreal, but I couldn't get in the mood to consider how I might spend the money.

I was alive—I survived—and I was exhausted. *How to use my heaps of money can wait until later.*

Hundreds of million yen really was an unreal prospect—so unreal, in fact, that it never came to be.

A few days after the dungeon clearing, news spread across Japan that Horinomiya Akihiro, Company President and CEO of Horimiya Group, had lost his whole fortune and was filing for bankruptcy.

2

A LLOW ME TO GIVE YOU A BRIEF OVERVIEW OF THE fate of Horinomiya Akihiro.

The company president and CEO of Horimiya Group had been hiring expensive parties of adventurers and supporting their operations in dungeon clearings all around the world, using his own personal funds like water. He had borrowed huge amounts of money from major banks using stocks in his own company as collateral. Several days after we explored the Omori Dungeon, the suspicious stock trading detailed on his latest large shareholder report was picked up by drama YourTubers and finance bloggers, who ran with it gleefully.

"Is the company president of Horimiya Group almost bankrupt?!"

The negative news spread quickly, and Horimiya Group's stock prices tanked. This caused a chain of consequences to occur. The sudden drop in the value of his collateral caused a reaction from the banks, much like a cup filling up with water that finally reached its breaking point and spilled over.

Horinomiya's entire fortune vanished overnight. He filed for bankruptcy and resigned from the Horimiya Group. All the businesses he had been involved in were handed over to different individuals, and after a few short days, he had lost everything he'd built.

Rumors began to spread of the extremely expensive dungeon resource he had recently come into possession of, a Blessing of Eir, and speculated about the item's whereabouts. Articles began to refer to him as "The Modern-Day Qin Shi Huang," as that emperor's quest for long life and immortality was not dissimilar to Horinomiya's descent into bankruptcy—but in the end, the item was never found. He insisted that in the confusion and chaos of the bankruptcy and his resignation, the Blessing of Eir was given away to a third party, but nobody believed him.

"But why would he continue to hide it?"

Nobody knew the answer to that question either. In the end, neither I nor the members of REA were able to squeeze our reward money from the now-bankrupt Horinomiya.

Several days had passed since all the commotion. I took my Celsiar out to a certain restaurant on the outskirts of Omori City after Carol gave me a certain tip. Lunchtime was over, and there were no other customers. I was shown to a table seat and looked at the menu, waiting for the waiter to return. I heard footsteps clicking towards me and saw a tall man standing by my table.

"What can I get you?" he asked.

He knew who I was, of course, but didn't think that fact particularly warranted mentioning here.

"I guess I'll have the steak."

"Understood."

"How are you?" I asked him.

"Well enough, I suppose," answered the handsome, later-middle-aged man with graying hair.

Horinomiya Akihiro, the former company president and CEO of Horimiya Group, one of Japan's leading businessmen, was now an employee at a small countryside restaurant.

Several days earlier...

"It's mere speculation," Carol told me over the phone.

In trying to extract their reward money from the bankrupt Horinomiya, members of REA made a number of interesting discoveries about the man's personal life. Horinomiya Akihiro was not married, but according to his former secretary, there was a possibility that he had a daughter. The secretary had heard from the man himself that the chances that this rumored daughter was his by blood were incredibly high.

Horinomiya was known for being a handsome businessman, but contrary to public perception, he had almost no relationships with women. But about ten years ago, there was a woman in his orbit—one with whom he shared a deep bond, for the first and only time in his life. The secretary unfortunately didn't know why the two of them did not marry, or why they lived apart.

The woman gave birth to a child soon after separating from him. She raised the girl as a single mother, completely apart from and unconnected to Horinomiya. It was that daughter that the businessman had said, apparently, was very likely to be his. Apparently he himself had a strong feeling that the girl was his daughter—he must have had a DNA test. His former secretary knew that he had ordered a private investigator to retrieve some of the girl's hair for sampling.

He never went to visit the girl's mother, but through his secretary and investigators, he was always gathering personal information about this potential daughter. There were long-focus lens pictures taken, reports on how she was doing in kindergarten, yearly infiltration of her elementary school culture festivals, and videos taken of the school plays in which she appeared. Horinomiya was said to treasure these. The former secretary said that aspect of him was almost like a sickness, and that only a select few of his most trusted subordinates knew the secret.

Not even his former secretary knew what he felt towards the girl, but she sensed that as a company man devoted entirely to his business, Horinomiya's life was both grand in scale but also somewhat barren. He lived his life in indifference—but the young girl was his one obsession.

When the girl was diagnosed with a heart condition and told she had only a few years to live, Horinomiya was apparently terribly shaken by the news. According to his former secretary, it was incredibly rare for anything to really affect him. It was immediately after the girl fell ill that the first dungeon, the NY Dungeon, appeared in the world, and roughly a year later, the Blessing of Eir was discovered in the United States. After that, Horinomiya devoted himself completely to locating another of that magical item, which was said to be capable of curing any and all illness.

It was the night before Horinomiya's bankruptcy that a young girl who had long been hospitalized with a heart condition suddenly made a complete recovery. The doctors were stumped. They had no idea how it had happened practically overnight—how could someone have gone from having only a few months to live to being completely cured? It was mindboggling.

After a while, Horinomiya returned to my table with a mouthwatering steak. He placed it before me and sat down opposite me, the same way he had the first time we'd met. He sat sideways on the chair, and I couldn't help but notice how long his legs were. I picked up my knife and fork and started to eat.

There was silence between us for a short while.

"Why?" I asked, at last. "Why did you threaten me?"

"I thought that would be the easiest solution," he said, still looking off to the side.

"I mean, if you explained all this to me, I would have acted differently."

"I have no idea what you're talking about," he replied.

"What was the point in lying like that?" I asked, referring to the way the world now saw him, the modern-day Qin Shi Huang, driven insane in his quest for immortality.

"That made everything easier to understand," he said. "There was no need to overcomplicate matters."

"You couldn't help but lie, then?"

"Everyone thinks that's just what rich people are. It's the easiest way for them to try to understand us. It's good when things are clear and easy to comprehend. It helps people focus on the things that they really need to focus on when matters are simplified."

He stared out the window, never turning his gaze towards me once. "We all wear our masks in this life," he continued. "We wear the ones that suit us the most, donning those that help us to maneuver as best we can. We believe those masks to be our true faces."

"I have no idea what you're getting at."

"I mean to say that this is the path I chose, the way I believe was best—and as a result of my decision to do the thing I wished to, this is what has transpired. That is all."

My cutlery clicked against the plate as I silently brought another bite of steak to my mouth. *This is delicious... Not that I know much about good steak, but I feel like there's some special kind of flavoring to one brought to you by a man who was, until a few days ago, a big leader in Japan's economy.*

"Allow me to apologize," Horinomiya suddenly started, cutting straight to the point. "As you well know, I'm now penniless. I cannot pay you the reward I promised."

"I figured as much."

"My apartment's rent is just 20,000 yen a month, but I can't even afford a washing machine. I truly have no money at present—though I do have plenty of debt."

"I know. I don't care about any of that now. The hundreds of millions of yen you promised us was all fake anyway, right from the start," I replied.

"Thank you for your understanding."

"But those are just my feelings on the matter." I put down my knife and fork with a *clink* and wiped my mouth with a napkin. "There are others who *do* care about the money."

It was then that I saw a look of shock on Horinomiya's face for the first time. But in the next moment, it was gone, and he seemed to have understood my words.

This guy did carry Japan's economy on his back until recently, after all. He's the real deal when it comes to brainpower.

The two well-built men who were sneaking up behind Horinomiya suddenly caught him by the shoulders. They were members of REA: one was the combat medic who *still* hadn't purchased an Auto-Translate skill, and the other was the shotgunner who had helped me out down in the dungeon.

The medic's English seemed polite this time. "Will you come with us for a minute, please?"

"I'd like you to accompany us, Horinomiya-san."

Horinomiya seemed to understand the situation, looking around silently as the two men took hold of his arms. A large van pulled up in the restaurant parking lot and came to a stop. We were both completely surrounded by REA members now—and with the cast fully assembled, the final player emerged from a corner of the restaurant.

"He's right. Some of us can't help but care about this," said a youthful, feminine voice. It was the REA captain Carol Middleton, who was slowly approaching Horinomiya from behind. "We always get our money. No matter what it takes."

Now completely surrounded by REA, Horinomiya's hands began to tremble. "What are you going to do with me?" he asked, looking at me.

I didn't respond. There was no pretense there—it was Carol's question to answer, not mine.

"Perhaps you had your own reasons for doing what you did. But there's too much money on the line for us to forgive you," she said. "You're coming with us, Horinomiya Akihiro. You'll be paying us our reward in a *different way*."

"A-are you going to purge me…?" Horinomiya's voice was trembling, imagining the worst fate that might await him.

Carol just looked at him—her eyes were cold. "What are you going to do if I tell you?"

"This is Japan. There's a rule of law."

"We're REA. We're not from here."

"Give up, Horinomiya," I said.

The man was pulled up from his chair by the two who had hold of his arms. I stood up and followed as they dragged him away. It wasn't that I wanted to do anything to him, but I wanted to burn the image of that grand, dignified man's final moments into my memory. The door of the black van there to kidnap him opened, like the darkness of a cave leading straight to hell.

Just before he was shoved inside, Horinomiya looked over at me. "Wait. Let me talk to him, just once more."

"There's no need for that," said Carol coldly.

"Wait, please. I need to tell him something. It's about the skillbook."

"About Skillbook?"

The REA members stopped trying to push him into the van and looked to Carol for orders. She touched her chin, and Horinomiya was sat down in the back with the two men on either side of him.

He turned to me. "Your rare skill...Skillbook..."

"Do you know something about it?" I asked.

Horinomiya dryly swallowed, then nodded. "I've traveled the world commissioning dungeon explorations. I once heard talk of a similar skill."

"A similar one?" I leaned forward, putting one foot into the back of the van.

"Yes," he said. "I don't know all the details...but it was said to be capable of activating skills in a different way. A nontypical way, I mean. Similar to the way in which your Skillbook can, except yours turns skills into cards."

Activating skills in a different way, huh? That does sound like the same type of thing that my skill does.

"Tell me more."

"I...I don't know any more than that. It's just a rumor I heard from someone, back when I was involved in the NY Dungeon exploration. Even the existence of that skill is off-the-record, and the American government has been keeping it under wraps ever since. I was told that they handed it over to Wallace. But these are all just rumors, of course."

Wallace... Wallace Chandler. He's the USA's former Level 100 man, the pride of that great country. Before the great level shift, he was the strongest man in the world, and even now he still tentatively holds the title.

"You don't know anything else?" I pressed.

"Just one more thing. That special skill... They say that its features evolve the more it's used."

"What do you mean?"

"Does such a skill really exist?" asked Carol. Her face was suddenly right there next to mine, listening closely to Horinomiya's words.

"From what I've heard, yes. So...it may be of the same type as yours. You may yet be able to draw more from that Skillbook you have. No, to put it more accurately...there could still be aspects of it which you're currently unable to bring out. It will grow and develop. It's possible that it is...locked, in some way."

I was silent for a moment, thinking about what he said. *Is this just him trying to put off his own kidnapping? A pack of lies for just a moment's respite? Maybe he's just trying to get us interested in what he has to say, no matter what. Or it's some way of bringing himself back to the negotiating table, raising the odds of his own salvation, whatever it takes.*

"Is that all you had to say?" asked Carol.

"Yes, that's all...Mizuki-kun," he said, looking at me now. "Spare me my life, won't you?"

"...Sorry," I said. "I think it's too late for that."

"Right then. Good work on extracting that information," said Carol, stepping back from the van. "Take him away."

I stepped back too, and the van's black doors closed. The moment before they shut completely my eyes met Horinomiya's— his were filled with terror.

I guess he never even dreamed this could happen to him—not in a country like Japan where there's a rule of law. There was a kind of detached air that he put on, as if he knew everything in the world—but he hadn't prepared himself for this. I guess he never expected to meet a fate worthy of some gang or mafia movie.

Everyone has a moment when they realize their own foolishness... I sure hope that for me, that moment comes before it's too late to fix everything.

The van's engine started up, and the heavy vehicle slowly pulled out onto an empty highway. I stood by Carol's side outside the restaurant, watching the van with the REA members and Horinomiya inside drive away, until it was out of sight.

"Right. That's taken care of now," said Carol, looking refreshed to be done with it.

"You want something to eat?" I asked.

"You've already had some steak, haven't you?"

"I've still got room," I said.

"All right. Let's get something."

Carol and I walked back towards the restaurant.

"So have you picked a channel name yet?" I asked.

"'Horimiya Channel' should do."

I suppose I need to add a brief addendum to the fate of Horinomiya Akihiro at this point. One week after our meeting at the restaurant, the former businessman and "Modern-Day Qin Shi Huang" Horinomiya Akihiro turned over a new leaf and started a YourTube channel.

The commotion around his bankruptcy had died down a little, but he was still a hot celebrity, so his channel got off to a fine start. There was a lot of chatter about it online. Critics and defenders argued about it, but his consistent uploads and unexpected and fresh content grew his fanbase. His subscriber count shot up at a record-breaking pace. It seemed like his calm demeanor, contrasted with his wild ideas and athletic stunts, gained him a lot of fans.

According to a YourTube critic in my social circle named Shinobu, what was so great about his videos was the perfect way in which you had absolutely no idea what he was thinking. Shinobu, of course, hadn't the slightest inkling that I had a hand in Horinomiya's YourTube debut, nor would she ever have dreamed that she herself was somewhat of an indirect influence on it.

I proposed the idea at a meeting with REA on how we might extract our unpaid reward money from the bankrupted Horinomiya.

"Hey, why don't we get him on YourTube or something?" I'd said, half as a joke, with Shinobu in the back of my mind.

Carol had jumped on the idea. "That's it."

Horinomiya had been convinced that he was going to be killed, so he was surprisingly cooperative when it came to filming videos.

I mean, I bet anyone in the world would rather make a living doing something they enjoy than be killed.

Part of the channel's ad revenue went towards paying off Horinomiya's debts and to his living expenses, but most of the rest was taken by REA to cover their unpaid rewards. The fact that REA was sponsoring Horimiya Channel was public information, and it served as both an advertisement for their activities in Japan as well as a continuous source of money. Every day, Kessie waited patiently for new Horimiya Channel videos to see what he'd be up to that day.

To be honest, given how interesting they were, I looked forward to them myself.

[Shocking] Horimiya suddenly attacked by macho special forces?! What's he going to do?! Surprise ending
605,495 Views   Posted 8 hours ago
👍 14k 👎 3400

TAKAHASHI 8 hours ago
BAD END for a former businessman
👍 203 👎 0
Display 17 replies ⌄

Masukara-san 5 hours ago
So funny that Horinomiya-san doesn't seem to want to be doing this lol
👍 54 👎 3

I like Gang Knu 3 hours ago
I liek Horimiya
👍 45 👎 1
Display 34 replies ⌄

Oriental TV Moving the Japanese Archipelago 1cm for Each Subscriber 8 hours ago
I love this channel!!!!!!!!
👍 0 👎 5

THE AVERTED HOKKAIDO DRAGON CRISIS

1

"**S**O ANYWAY... MIZUKI, COME JOIN US AT REA. OFFICIALLY." Carol was facing me, the two of us sitting at a small round table in her hotel room.

"Nah," I said. "I'm not even British, you know? I'm Japanese."

"That doesn't matter. Sports teams around the world hire foreign players all the time." Carol elegantly pushed a can of coffee towards me—she probably bought it from one of the hotel's vending machines. *Drink*, the gesture seemed to say. "If you join us at REA, you'll have an opportunity to test out the way that Skillbook of yours works using a wide variety of different skills."

"Hmm..." I scratched my cheek and thought about the proposal.

Carol continued, however, without giving me any time to reflect. "It would give you economic stability as well. Work for us for a year and you could build yourself a fine fortune. As a member of REA, we could protect you and Miss Kessie. We can offer you high-level security, even if you do leave us in the future. We know a great deal about the adventuring world and have unique connections all around the globe too."

"Hmmmm..."

"What more could you even ask for?" she asked, honestly confused.

Well, getting scouted by the number-one adventuring party in the UK was an honor, especially when they were saying they needed me like this. I bet a lot of adventurers fantasized about moments like this—lucky breaks that never come. But joining REA might mean I have to go public with Kessie. Of course, keeping her hidden for the rest of my life didn't sound easy either, but I supposed I could come to an understanding with Kessie about it... but it worried me a little.

Also, becoming the most famous and successful adventurer in Japan would make me one heck of a celebrity, the kind that TV stations would send fleets of reporters out to talk to... *That* was the kind of person this decision could turn me into. I wondered about that, and what it'd be like. For anyone else, this could be a lucky break, but I didn't really have that self-affirming drive that other people did... Or rather, I tried to avoid it when I could.

I needed a bit more time to think it over.

"Then what is it you want, Mizuki?" Carol asked. "Tell me your demands."

"It's not that," I said. "I don't have any real demands... I just need more time to think about it. I haven't talked that much to Kessie about this, for starters."

Carol offered up some ideas to me. "Money? Women? Other accommodations?"

"I mean, yeah, of course I want all those things. Wait, what do you mean by women, anyway? One of those things isn't like the others."

"I've been told that men want women. That is all."

"Sounds like a universal truth to me, but I think you might be using it wrong there," I said.

"REA can provide you with everything."

"Not women, though."

"There's me."

"What?"

Carol gazed at me, her expression absolutely serious. "You aren't satisfied with me?"

"I...see. So *that's* what you meant. I should correct that little misunderstanding there..." I started. "Most men want love, marriage... They're after the opposite sex for, uh, ulterior motives... They don't want women in the sense of just working for and alongside them. That's...not quite what the phrase means. I think. Probably. Keep that in mind."

My confidence in the statement I made was already starting to fade, even though I was the one who said it in the first place. *What am I even trying to explain? It sounds like there's a lot she doesn't know about the world, so it kind of makes me want to start these lessons right from the beginning.*

"So why *not* me?" Carol asked again, sitting sideways on the chair. She draped an arm over the back of it and rested her hand on the top. Since the dungeon incident, where almost all of her armor was broken, she bought herself a new set of lightweight gear. Apparently it was from some other dungeon, and it gave her a buff for wearing the full set.

But if you asked me what changed about her appearance, I honestly don't think I could tell you. It was like something changed, but also not really. It was like a subtle change in a woman's hairstyle, or the really minor changes that certain American comic book heroes' suits would have from movie to movie... Really small alterations only a real nerd would pick up on.

That being said, the black cloth that covered the area between her legs completely had a few more openings to give the outfit room to breathe now. She was showing a lot more skin below the waist than before. *Pathetic as it is to admit, men might not notice a change in hairstyle, but a little more exposed skin? They can pick up on that down to the last millimeter.*

"What are you saying?" I asked.

"Listen, Mizuki. I intend for you to join REA and ultimately become my husband in the future. Men and women can marry at the age of sixteen in the UK, and I am already sixteen years old."

"Yeah, I still have no idea what you're getting at here."

I was so bewildered by what she was saying that I turned into the poet Aida Mitsuo.

Young, blonde-haired, blue-eyed girls sure do say some weird things. —Mizuki.

"I found you. Ever since that day, three years ago...I've always found everything I needed to survive down in the dungeons. This time, I found Horinomiya, a powerful advertisement for REA's activities, and an unrivalled consultant on financial matters."

The former businessman managed a fine transition into his new rookie YourTuber role, even though it was forced upon him, and it sounded like Horinomiya Akihiro was still working as PR and financial advisor for REA to pay off his remaining debts. I did ask if he was okay with all this, but apparently the field of work suited him, and it was turning into a surprisingly good partnership for all parties. It looked like he intended to withdraw completely from society after his bankruptcy, refusing contact with anyone and living quietly in the shadows for the rest of his days. To him, right now, it's like Horinomiya Akihiro had already died once. I figured his point was, "I'm already dead, so make whatever use of me you like."

Apparently, when he first started making those YourTube videos as repentance, he wanted to quit. It was a pretty dangerous situation for a while... But once he learned that a certain girl who was almost certainly his true daughter was a devoted fan of the videos, his resistance faded. I guess he must have managed to find her YourTube account somehow. She left comments sometimes, and she was the only one whose comments he'd like and respond to.

An unexpected, hidden side to him... In any case, he seemed to be doing well.

"Most of all, I've found a husband now in the depths of the Omori Dungeon. You're the best loot I've ever gotten. I could *never* give you up." Carol nodded to herself. "You've got a likeable personality, and I have no complaints when it comes to your abilities. The true strength and nature of a person are only ever revealed in the extremes of a dungeon. Down there, you proved yourself to me... You showed me that you're fit to be my husband, and I am fit to be your wife. Join REA. Become mine."

"..."

Was this that switch of hers? The one the other REA members talked about? I talked to them after we left the dungeon to get more details about Carol's experiences. She was pushed to her absolute limits, down there alone in the depths of that dungeon three years ago, and she had to survive on dungeon resources alone for three whole days... Dungeons have become a kind of trigger for her moods, and they made her very, *very* excitable.

"Your expression seems strained. What isn't to your liking?" she asked.

"Um...look. Uh... I feel like there's a whole lot I'd like to say right now..."

Carol laughed at how flustered I was. "I have an idea of what you're worried about. I'm very aware of the nature of you *men*, of course. I won't stand with custom and demand that you wait until I come of age for us to develop *that kind* of a relationship. Don't worry, the age of consent in the UK is sixteen years old. I know what to do, also. I'm busy with my work as an adventurer so can't attend secondary school, but I take classes at an online school, and I've learned some things from books."

Yeesh. Doesn't sound like she knows anything about the bad stuff.

"Or...is that you don't want to be with *me*?" she asked.

"No, that's not it."

"You hate British people? You don't like our politics?"

"No. That's not it either."

"You don't like the way I look, then?" she offered.

I'm kind of limited by the age gap between us, but she is super cute, to be honest.

"You saw me naked as well," she continued. "You've got a responsibility to protect my virtue now, to keep it intact."

"You were naked in front of one of the other party members too," I pointed out.

"No I wasn't."

"That combat medic. I never know what he's saying, but he saw you. He gave you his clothes, remember?"

"Kevin's gay," she said.

Oh. Right.

"In any case, you just need to join REA, come with us back to the UK, and that will solve everything. Understood?"

"Understood," I replied. "So let's put this on hold for now."

"Why?!" She was suddenly acting her age, but it only lasted a moment. "Anyway. You mentioned that you had to enter Omori Dungeon again, didn't you?" she asked.

"I guess I did, yeah."

"I'll go with you, so go ahead and put in the application. You didn't think I'd agree to be your wife without a date first, did you?"

I mean, you basically did say that... Anyway, I also think I'd be the first person in Japan to go on a date in a dungeon...

2

I MADE SEVERAL ATTEMPTS TO FIND CLOTHES FOR Kessie. I visited toy stores like Toys "B" Us to buy dolls that you could take the clothes off of. I even found a few pieces online that were meant for dolls and figures, but each time...

"Ghaaaah! It's so itchy! It's really, really itchy! Itchy off the freakin' scale!!!"

And so, with none of the doll clothes being comfortable enough, I still hadn't found anything that Kessie could wear. It was then that Carol and the other members of REA came to the rescue using one of their contacts. They had a set of fairy clothes specially made, and in fact, the package had just arrived.

"Whoa! Amaziiiing!!!" said Kessie, taking the clothes out of their little case and holding them up.

"Hmm... Those look nice..."

"These clothes are incredible!!! Waah! Can I really keep them?!"

Nobody else in the world can wear them but you.

Kessie's clothing didn't look anything like normal people would wear. Instead, it was more like a skintight suit you might see someone from the future wearing in a science-fiction movie. The material was stretchy and elastic. When Kessie put it on, the sizing was so perfect that even with the fabric hugging her body, her silhouette still looked like she was naked.

"Oh! This is really great! Super, amazingly good!!!"

Well, good for you.

Apparently, it was pretty expensive even to just make one of these. Even so, the standout MVP of that last dungeon clearing was Kessie, so she deserved it. She did everything from navigating, to helping us communicate, to helping me fight that monster—even with that small of a body. I still didn't feel like the reward I gave her was enough as all she got was this suit and a *How About Thursday?* DVD box set. But hey, if she ever wanted anything else, I planned on getting it for her.

Kessie's new bodysuit also had a practical purpose. It could hide the soft glowing light her skin was constantly giving off. Sure, it only hid the parts of her skin the suit itself actually covered, but it was better than nothing.

Right, then. I checked my watch. *10:20... It's about time.*

I wanted to hurry up and deliver my batteries to that dragon, so I was set to dive into the Omori Dungeon once more with Carol. I applied for a spot in advance and finally got a reservation for twelve o'clock today.

I figured it would be easier to get all this done once the office managing the dungeon was up and running, but at the moment, it was still a bit difficult to get all the paperwork done. In any case, we were going by car, so I knew Carol would be arriving soon.

Sure enough, just then, the doorbell rang.

That must be her.

I went to open the door, but instead of Carol standing outside,

I found Shinobu there, wearing her usual hoodie. She waved at me, convenience store bubble tea in one hand.

"Sup, Mizuki-san."

"H-hey, Shinobu... What is it?"

"You didn't respond to me on Lain so I came over."

Most of the Lain messages I received on any given day were from Shinobu, so I had turned off my notifications. It wasn't like I was *completely* ignoring her, but I couldn't respond to everything she sent either.

"Am I interrupting something?"

"No... Not quite. Why aren't you at school today?"

Shinobu had told me that her suspension was over and she was attending school again.

And that sure is a weird T-shirt she's got on under her hoodie...

Her zipper was open wide, exposing some of her chest.

"School holiday today."

"Oh, right. Um..."

"Want to play some games?" she asked. "I brought my Stitch."

"Ah, well... Sorry, but I've got some errands to take care of."

"Oh really? That's a shame. What kind of errands?"

"You know. Regular errands..." I said, trailing off.

"What do you mean *regular* errands?"

She's quite the detective, huh...

Then, I heard footsteps on the staircase that led to my apartment. It turned out those actually *were* Carol this time.

"Mizukiii! I'm here! Should I wait in the car, or...?"

Carol reached the top of the stairs and saw Shinobu standing in front of my door—Shinobu in that unzipped hoodie, and Carol in her set of lightweight dungeon armor.

The two of them stared at each other for a moment.

Huh? This isn't one of those kind of...weird situations, is it?

A few seconds passed, then they both spoke at the same time.

"Mizuki. Let's go."

"Who is she, Mizuki-san?"

"Uh... Shinobu, Carol. Carol, Shinobu."

Shinobu narrowed her eyes at the other young woman. She took another sip from the thick straw stuck into her bubble tea and glanced over at me. "Your 'errand'... It's with her, then?"

"Yeah." *No point in lying about that.*

"What is it, Mizuki? Let's go," Carol urged me again.

So that's how Carol is with this kind of stuff. She doesn't even notice it happening. But Shinobu...she's really bothered by this situation. It's not like I'm doing anything wrong right now... Wait. Am I in the wrong here? What?

These unsettling thoughts were still floating through my head as my neighbor opened the door.

"Mizuki? I want you to show me how to do something, do you have time?"

It was Heath, the foreigner who lived next door.

You're crashing this party now too, eh? Now this is getting complicated. Wait, no... Should I be really happy that Heath is joining the conversation?

"Ah... Sorry, I'm just about to head out. I have something to do," I replied.

"Oh," he said. "Will you be free once you're home?"

"What do you need me to show you?"

"The American Department of Defense, I think it's called... I want to know about their security... I don't get how this Google search thing works though."

What are you interested in that *for? You can't get that kind of intel from an internet search. Seriously, how do you make your money?*

"Mizuki, we're leaving," said Carol.

"Hmm... I see, I see. So you've got an *errand* with *her* then, Mizuki-san."

"Mizuki, please teach me about this Google search stuff once you're back. Is it expensive?"

Hmm... This situation sure has gotten a lot more hectic all of a sudden. But hey, things have calmed down now, haven't they? All I really know is that there's a scaly, ice-type client waiting for that delivery I promised him, so I need to go.

And so, after dodging Heath and Shinobu, Carol and I headed off towards the Omori Dungeon once more.

3

THE STRUCTURE BEING BUILT AT THE OMORI Dungeon was still under heavy construction. A lot more had been done since our last visit, but adventurers were still only barely allowed inside. The real work on the entrance was about to begin, which meant entry would be closed for a short while—though adventurers would still be allowed inside with the right permissions and if they were accompanied by a staff director and construction worker.

There was a more complicated and drawn-out process in place for bringing firearms restricted by Japanese law into the dungeons, but we had no need of them this time.

Outside, there were two prefabricated buildings about the size of bathrooms for people to change in—one for men, one for women. It was in those that we completed our final preparations before entering the dungeon.

As I changed, I remembered the conversation I had with Carol in the car on our way here.

"What was the matter with your neighbor, Mizuki?" she asked, her big sports bag sitting on her lap.

"He's a little weird, but I don't really have a clear idea of what he does for work."

"My Scale Eyes couldn't analyze him."

"Huh? What do you mean?" I asked.

"I tried getting some intel on him as I always do, but the information wouldn't come up. I think he must have some passive skill preventing his stats from being read."

"Do those kinds of skills really exist?"

"Very few. The most elite of elite adventurers sometimes have Interference Skills on hand to block people analyzing them...but I've rarely met anyone using one. Who *is* he?" Carol asked.

I wasn't sure how to answer her question at the time.

I want to sit down and ask him properly sometime.

When I left the changing room, Carol was already waiting for me outside.

"You're late, Mizuki. Let's go."

"Wait," I blurted out. "What's *that*? What are you wearing?"

"I had some special new gear prepared for me," she said. "It's for you."

Carol wasn't wearing her normal lightweight armor anymore. Instead, she had changed into a set of armor that looked fairly typical of women in Japanese fantasy games—and it put quite a lot on display.

Does it need to be so...lewd? Doesn't all the exposed skin make it far less protective than regular armor? I bet I could spend an hour questioning her about her outfit. What's the point in accentuating the butt and chest in the design? What's the practical purpose there?

I turned my head to the side, wondering if it even qualified as armor or if it was just a bikini.

Well, I did wonder why her sports bag was rattling so much... So this is what she had in there.

Carol spun where she stood to show it off to me. The design, for some reason, deliberately exposed her underarms and belly button, and seemed like it was sorely lacking in protective capabilities. The chest plate drew attention to her breasts, and the bit covering her backside was less a piece of armor and more a deliberate attempt to show off her butt. There was suspiciously little cloth poking out underneath too—she was basically wearing a thong below it.

"What do you think?" she asked. "Does it suit me? Men like this kind of thing, don't you?"

"Are you serious right now?"

"I didn't think you'd be so against this... That just hurts my feelings. I had this arranged because I thought it would make you happy."

"Ah. Right. I'm sorry." I apologized—Carol looked too upset. "But just to ask, is there any practical reason that the armor's like... that?" I asked.

"No. It keeps me cool, but that's all. Perfect to keep sunstroke at bay."

"You really should change back into your old armor."

Following Kessie's guidance, Carol and I proceeded through the dungeon—with Carol now dressed in her regular armor. The

Omori Dungeon had mostly goblins and a few slimes on the upper levels, so Carol was able to take care of them using her buffs and not needing to resort to Attack Skills. When it seemed safe, I fought too, testing out my Skillbook in combat.

"I really learned the importance of Contact Skills in our last battle," said Carol. She had just taken down four goblins that attacked us. "I need to rethink my battle strategies."

"What are Contact Skills?"

"Skills that give debuffs to the enemy on contact, even if that contact doesn't cause damage. They can be convenient; you should get one too."

"How much do they go for?"

"Anywhere from several to ten million yen. There are a lot of options."

"Figures," I said. "That's a heck of a lot of money."

I might've been willing to spend that much in a game, but in the real world, I didn't feel up to splurging in a weapons shop. That said, I did get a fairly big advance from Horinomiya for our mission, and I wanted to get my hands on a skill like that.

Right then. The more observant among you might have already noticed it, but here we are, after all the twists and turns, right back at the beginning of our story. We began our marathon at the Omori branch of Showa Securities, and now we're back here for our first little break.

That said, to tell the brief tale of one Mizuki Ryosuke (myself) will be something that takes us much further into the future. I've only just started running this endurance marathon and have yet to reach anything that might come close to being called a conclusion.

But eventually, that day *will* come.

Kessie, Heath, Shinobu, Horinomiya, Carol. I've met all these people, but they've yet to show me their true natures. Some of them I still can't understand at all. I, Mizuki Ryosuke, have truly stumbled upon an unusual, eccentric, and extravagant world...

Someday, I'll tell you how all of this really ends. But for now, this is simply a break point. There should be something appropriate here for us while we take our break, shouldn't there? And as for the vague details of this world—I want to leave that explanation to our scaly white friend.

Proceeding through the caves, we found a hidden passageway that only Kessie could detect. Stepping inside, I felt the cold air on my skin giving me goosebumps all over. At the end of that passage was a familiar, snowy cave.

When Carol and I stepped inside, the great white dragon stirred, and raised its head up from its slumber with a rumbling sound.

<Mizuki... Mizuki Ryosuke! I've waited an age for you to come! What took you so long?!>

"I'm so sorry to have kept you waiting!" I shouted back, a little happy to see him.

After all, it was an emotional reunion with my first-ever dungeon client.

4

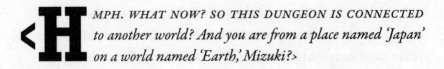

<Hmph. What now? So this dungeon is connected to another world? And you are from a place named 'Japan' on a world named 'Earth,' Mizuki?>

The white dragon seemed pleased with his mountain of AA batteries, letting out puffs of snow with every breath as he panted happily.

"That's right," I told the dragon. "At least, I believe so, yes. The world which you and Kessie hail from is different from mine, noble dragon... Something seems to have happened to connect the two... I think."

Kessie did a few more midair bows next to me in her new suit, helping me explain. Carol stood frozen to the spot—it seemed she hadn't truly believed that the dragon I met was quite so large.

I did explain it to her...but maybe she thought I was joking about this.

I continued addressing the dragon. "And, well, Kessie seems to think that perhaps...you might know some way of returning to your old world, noble dragon..."

<It cannot be done,> he replied.

"It can't?" I asked.

"Um, well... Do you mean to say there's no way to get through this dungeon and back to the old world?" asked Kessie.

<That is not my meaning.> The dragon lightly shook his head, then turned his white scaly eyes on me. <It is likely that the old world no longer exists.>

"Huh?"

"Huuh???"

Kessie and I reacted at the same time.

<I see, I see... So that's the situation, then. My, my. I did have my suspicions.> The dragon nodded to himself, accepting it all. <The human and monster races fought for ages in that world, with civilizations built on magic. But now it is finished. I watched as they walked

their paths for so long, but in ages past, I found myself bored of them and buried myself in this endless dungeon. It saddens me to think that now they are gone.>

"Ahem, so... What do you mean?" asked Kessie.

<I mean to say that world is gone. Finished. Vanished without a trace,> said the dragon. His tone was like that of a teacher speaking to a difficult student. *<All that remains is this labyrinth, which through some twist of fate has now stuck its nose into your world, nothing more. Everything that once was in that world—all its strength, all the fragments of those that existed there... Now they are scattered and fallen with no one to clean them up. That is simply what has happened... I had suspected it for some time, but now I know for certain.>*

"I'm sorry," I said, "but this is a bit too abstract for me... I don't quite understand what you're saying."

<Is there truly any need for you to understand? No one understands. When no solution can be reached, nothing can come of understanding—perhaps harm is a more likely result. What salvation would there be in understanding the fate of two worlds heading for inescapable ruin? Would you not be much happier falling asleep tonight in ignorance, than in full knowledge that tomorrow the world will come to an end?>

"Ruin? We're going to die tomorrow?" I reflexively took a step forward. "What do you mean?"

I was starting to feel like what he was telling us might be incredibly important—something I absolutely had to take in.

The white dragon turned his head a little to the side. There was a hint of sadness in the way he narrowed his snake-like eyes at me.

<When one end of a bridge falls, those in the middle of it will no doubt make for the other side. They must make it across before the

whole bridge collapses. The big ones in the depths of this place will try to invade your world in search of safe land and rest. One has already found its way over, in fact.>

"Have they?"

<Yes indeed. It was the moment before their world vanished. The very one who connected the two, in fact. The Black One who broke that world in order to connect them, to bring it all to an end.>

The dragon suddenly seemed to grow tired, and, lowering himself to the ground, began to coil up.

<I had to clear the way to avoid it as it made its way up to the surface, so I moved here for the time being. It was the passage of that thing through our homes that so confused and scrambled the order of this place.>

"Um... What does that mean? Could you tell me a little more about this thing that passed through...?"

<I have talked for too long, been awake too long, and now I am sleepy,> the dragon said. *<I am relieved to have so many batteries now. Soon, I must sleep, and sleep for a long time. I will wake again before this place is gone.>*

"Excuse me, but if we could just discuss this a little longer..." I began.

<Mizuki, I will seal this place so that none can interrupt my slumber. I know you do not wish to be inside here when that happens, so leave now,> the dragon said. *<Thank you for the batteries.>*

"Ah, well... I'm so sorry I kept you waiting so long for the delivery..."

<Hmph. Had you been a little later in coming, I might have chosen to leave this dungeon and venture into the outside world to find you.>

Wait—Hokkaido almost had a dragon crisis just because I got busy and put off coming down here? That was close!

<Well then, Mizuki. See you in a thousand, or perhaps a couple of thousand years.>

Please don't span whole millennia like you're setting an alarm clock for seven or eight in the morning!

<Bring me more batteries when I wake... Mmh...>

There was no way I could offer *that* much of an extended warranty.

With our goal completed and having inadvertently prevented dragon warning sirens from blaring all across Hokkaido, Carol and I left the dungeon.

How can I put this? I thought the whole Horinomiya incident was pretty big, but in terms of its impact on the world, this day trip to deliver some batteries was way more important. If I was any later with the delivery, we would've seen a fight between the JSDF and a dragon. Or maybe an American Airforce vs. Ice Dragon showdown—a kaiju battle for the history books.

Was it really okay that things worked out this way? The whims of powerful beings like those were terrifying.

At the very least, it was a lesson learned for me—never keep your clients waiting if you can help it.

"What... What *was* that thing...?" asked Carol, sitting beside me in the passenger seat. Ever since our meeting with the dragon, she seemed stunned, as if she was still taking all of it in.

I explained it to her beforehand, but hearing about something was way different than seeing it with your own eyes. In any case, if that white dragon was going to be asleep for the next millennium, it was a load off my mind. The Hokkaido Dragon Crisis had been put off, at least for now. When we left the dragon, he was sealing himself in already, and we couldn't return to his cave anymore.

I thought over the dragon's words as we waited at a red light. There was still a mountain of things for me still to chew over.

That Heath guy who lives next door... I need to talk to him. But let's take this one step at a time.

But as you might expect, one never really *does* get much time to slowly think things over. The spark of the next conflict was already drawing close.

In fact, it was an individual I *already met* that was now trying to fan the flames.

A NOTE FROM THE
AUTHOR

"**W**OULDN'T IT BE FUNNY IF, LIKE, YOUR COMPANY office got turned into a dungeon, and you had to explore the thing just to clock in to work?"

"That'd be funny, lol."

That's basically how this novel came to be.

I'm not great at thinking up a plot beforehand—like the bones of the story, the path that characters will take—and in this work, I really think that aspect of my writing showed itself. I didn't have any steel rails in mind for the story to progress down, so it became a bit more of a free hike through the mountains without a path or any real goal. I did my best to keep up the pace, writing as hard as I could, though I did have a vague idea of where the story was going.

The environments in which I do my writing haven't been on the rails either. This work was originally posted on a website named *Shosetsuka ni Narou* ("Let's Be Novelists") and exploded in momentum (but mostly because of how fast I was posting). Just as we were heading into the Horinomiya arc, though, I had to fly off to Akita.

I couldn't exactly stop posting then, so during my Akita trip, I kept writing the Horinomiya arc and remembered to post.

On the last day, there was a typhoon that hit the town, and all the public transport went down, and I wasn't able to get home. There was nothing I could do but shut myself up in my hotel room and keep writing.

I think at that point I had just finished the Horinomiya arc... but I could be wrong.

Perhaps there are some readers here who have come from my other work, *Welcome to the Outcast's Restaurant!* Some of you might be surprised at the different tone in this one. This story is, in some ways, a result of the reaction to my previous one. As to what kind of reaction that was, I'll leave it up to your imagination.

In any case, volume one of this book has now been published. Thank you to everybody who helped and supported me in putting this book out. Thank you to my editor Y-sama, to CruelGZ-sama for the illustrations, and to T-sama who is editing the manga version. I don't know how this will be advertised when it comes to print, so I can only say that much for now.

Finally, thank you to all of my readers who supported this work as I posted it online. I hope we can meet again in the next volume.

Farewell!!!